# CONTENTS

*Ten Tales of the Tinier Type*

*page*

# BY WAY OF INTRODUCTION ...

## *... and explanation*

Following on is not something we cricketers volunteer to do but here is an exception, as this collection of literary trivialities indeed follows on from my effort: *"Good Morning, Sir George"*. [2020].

Once again, I gave myself the task of producing ten  short stories [in some cases -very short], all of which would share the same starting and closing words but would be set in different times, different places and with different - but perhaps in some ways similar -persons called "Sir George".

The demise of CompletelyNovel.com led me to the renowned Ingram Spark for a publication platform and my thanks are hereby acknowledged for their help and once again to the talented Jessica Barrah for yet another eye-catching cover.

As with my previous publication, this is not just a vanity exercise, for the royalties from this work will all go to the RNLI. In my attempt to provide fiction with a background of fact, I have drawn upon material assembled  from many sources which I duly acknowledge in a postscript to each Tale. I  hope that this little collection of "What possibly might have been" tales might raise a smile as you while away a rainy afternoon.

DONALD YULE

St Leonard's On Sea, East Sussex donyule@the-pres.org.uk

*Second in the* Sir George *Series*

# GOOD AFTERNOON, SIR GEORGE

## Another Ten Tales of the Tinier Type

## from

## Donald Yule

*Author of* Good Morning Sir George [2020]

ISBN  978 1 5272 8875 1



Typeset in Baskerville Old Face and Tahoma by the author.

The author thanks the following for their comments &  helpful suggestions whilst compiling these Tales:  Mary & Andy Barr; Chrissy Brand; Terry Critchley; Dave Lea; John Lovesey; Esther Lyons; Neb Peberdy; Gary Rolfe; Jim Willerton

# MARCH 1922

"Good Afternoon, Sir George."
The greeting from the serried ranks of clerks and lady typists came, without exception, in tones of total astonishment. *It was Friday afternoon!* Sir George was never to be seen in the office on a Friday afternoon!

As he passed through and into his office, an unprecedented murmur of chatter arose that was immediately silenced upon Miss Jones, who ruled the room with a rod of iron, calling for a prompt cessation and return to the standard hush. She then knocked upon the door of Sir George's office and upon the invitation, entered that "holy-of - holies". As she did so, her manner changed from the authoritarian to the deferential in keeping with being in the presence of one of the City of London's most highly respected financial figures.

"Is there something amiss, Sir George?"
"Miss Jones, I am sorry to startle you all with this sudden departure from habit but I am here at the behest of my wife and I have a task for you which will not wait till Monday."
" All is well with the Bank?"
"Heavens, there is no need for alarm there but my wife and her cook have come up with an idea which may lead to business."
"My goodness! How unusual!"
"Indeed but let me summarise. As you know, most days I am driven home from here or my Club by Hamilton. He is, as you have doubtless discerned, a most enterprising fellow – his War record testifies to that – and we are in the habit of passing through Cricklewood in north London on

the way home. In the last month, he has made a habit of stopping when he spies a particular horse and cart vendor and buying this local product called potato crisps – they come in bags at tuppence a time. He finally persuaded me to sample one and I agreed with him that they are a most ingenious little snack. I ended taking some home. My wife thinks them to be an excellent recipe for fried potato and remarkably nourishing but she felt they needed salt. Problem is that people do not carry salt around with them."

"It would be very difficult to sell salt alongside the potato slices as salt absorbs water."

"Exactly! So wife and cook experimented with putting some salt in a toffee wrapper and it would seem to solve the problem. I am sure that addition to the bag would make an enormous difference to sales. Hence I was directed to contact the manufacturer with that idea and the ever-resourceful Hamilton found them at the back of the Cricklewood Hotel would you believe. They have got as far as forming a limited company to trade but they look ripe for some capitalisation  and it has always been my policy to strike while the iron's hot. Hence, please take a letter, Miss Jones."

 The pair assumed their well-practised dictation routine and Sir George, hands together, fingertip to fingertip and with his gaze fixed ceiling-wards, began.

"Make it to The Managing Director Smiths Potato Crisps Ltd., Cricklewood London whatever – I am sure you can look that up - something along the lines of:

> *Dear Sir, I have recently been introduced to your product the 'potato crisp' and can vouch for your contention that it is most efficacious in relieving*

*pangs of hunger and is an easily digestible snack or possible accompaniment to savoury dishes.*

Paragraph:

*I believe this product to have a great future BUT currently is rather lacking flavour. The bag clearly needs some salt. Obviously if you include loose salt in the bag it will all collect in the base and will not adhere to the potato crisps. My wife and her domestic staff have experimented a little and have hit upon an efficacious method of including salt in a packet. May I suggest you include a small wax paper wrap with a portion of table salt. With this edition, I am certain the attractiveness of your unique product will increase.*

Paragraph - finally – to business:

*I note from Companies House that you had a start-up capital of £10,000 which you may well find to be inadequate if your enterprise expands as I believe it will. My bank would be pleased to consider financing your future growth and trust you will remember this letter when the need for further capital arrives.*

I am 'Yours etc' and sign it pro & per please in the usual way."

"Of course Sir George", replied Miss Jones, still rather startled by the situation.

" Bank's best stationery I think and, if you can get that typed up and in the last post, Miss Jones, I will have good tidings to take to Her Ladyship."

Later, relaxing in the leather upholstery of the Rolls Royce as Hamilton drove him homewards – without, on this occasion, stopping to buy the product whose  attractiveness had caused such a deviation from his normal habits – he experienced an unusual sense of satisfaction. It occurred to him, that when he got home, in response to the habitual query: *"Have you had a good day at the office?"* he would, for probably the first time ever, be able  to relate some business details which she could understand. It had been very strange but it had been a GOOD AFTERNOON

## AUTHOR'S POSTSCRIPT

We learn from Maurice Baren's fascinating *How It All Began, The Stories Behind Those Famous Names* [Smith Settle 1992] that thinly sliced potatoes cooked in oil were a local speciality of north London in the 1910's. The idea had occurred to Frank Smith, a manager in a London wholesale grocery company when his boss acquired a French recipe. Marketed as "potato crisps" and handmade, they sold at tuppence per bag from horse-drawn carts but Smith's employers were not enthusiastic about the product so he branched out on his own and in 1920, in co-operation with Joe Viney and George Ensor, formed Smith's Potato Crisps Ltd. With working capital behind the business and production on industrial lines, albeit on a small scale to start with behind the Crown Hotel [now the Clayton Crown Hotel]  in Cricklewood, London NW2, the enterprise prospered. Baren suggests that 1922 saw the introduction of that blue paper twist containing salt which fast became the trademark but the genesis of the idea remains undisclosed.
The subsequent commercial evolution is a tangled tale but I would suggest that the current derivatives of that product which first tickled our Sir George's palate remain as tasty.

# APRIL 2015

*"Good afternoon, Sir George."*

*Yes!* thought Susan, thumping the steering wheel of her parked car as she rehearsed the way she would shortly greet her ex-husband. *That's what I'll call him. And I'll really lay on the "Sir"! Because the cheating B will only be a 'sir' for a few days more until the Queen signs that piece of paper!* She took a swig from the bottle of spa water then gathered her thoughts. Then she put them into words and spoke them out loud, continuing the process of lecturing herself she had learnt in Rehab sessions.

"No - perhaps not – don't be vindictive Susan! All that is in the past. Show him who I am now – Susan  Caldicott, Charity Administrator from Purley  - Recovering Alcoholic – soon to be a qualified Accounting Technician - the one who drives her own car and has a good steady job with a real purpose -not that silly cow with the big boobs that  he married."
She shook her head in surprise at her own words and spoke out loud as though to the passing traffic.
"Yes - you said it Susan – 'silly cow'!"
*What a fool she had been!*

She had learnt not to spend time "beating herself up" over her errors and misjudgements but perhaps this was the time for one  last review before her impending visit slammed shut the book of her past life. She reached into the glove compartment, took out a tube of fruit pastilles and gave herself to a few minutes of reflection.

Chapter One in that book would have been her leaving the frugal environment of her  home and leading a very self-indulgent life  in and around Soho. Living in dingy flat shares, she was  precariously financed by part-time jobs in pubs and clubs and boring spells as a "publicity girl" smiling and handing out leaflets, occasionally flaunting her widely admired cleavage as a "hostess". Then – out of the blue - an Endowment Policy, bought and paid for by her ever-thrifty parents, matured and allowed her to display the cleavage to a more well-heeled strata of society.

Chapter Two would have been that  first meeting when she had been hired by an agency – a rather dubious one – to be a "Hostess" at a party for a City Whiz kid – someone called "Golden George". With her were two rather well-used "hostesses", "Rusty" and "Flinty" – both approaching their sell-by-date - who kept their kit on in atmosphere of drink and drugs  to which she was not used. She had done a strip then passed out, to  wake up hours later in a luxury penthouse flat. A rather pleasant looking young man with a nice quiet voice with an accent she recognised as polite Scottish was tending to her welfare. He looked and sounded like someone you could trust and re-introduced himself as "George".

Susan switched her memory on to "Fast Forward". It seemed like he cared for her so she trusted him and duly became his mistress, revelling in the life- style and the presents he bestowed upon her and the exotic locations they travelled to on holiday. The years seemed to flash past in the glitter and glamour of life as the consort of a star Fund Manager whom the press had nicknamed "Golden George". But she remembered that she regularly derided her school- teachers who had predicted that nothing would come of the idle day- dreaming girl who offered favours to boys at the back of the bike sheds in exchange for money or cigarettes.

Chapter Three would have started when "Golden George" announced that he was off on his own and, in a press fanfare, launched a new investment fund. But at the time, Susan detected no change to the lifestyle and so took little notice of her partner's business affairs. *Bother chapters!* thought Susan but the next milestone would have been when, *-gosh was it 2007?* - suddenly, George announced that it would be a good move to get officially married. Susan's expectations of a grand affair were to be very quickly dashed by George's words; "*It'll be good for business dear – no fuss*" and it was a very low-key affair at a local Registry Office. She remembered feeling odd that she should have been happy but wasn't.

*Another milestone*: later that Autumn, she remembered a morning when George suddenly came running through their luxury flat to where she was sitting doing a word puzzle. He was waving a very grand looking letter  and yelling her name as though there was something wrong. He leapt about in front of her punching the air and giving one of his very rare Scottish war whoops then – even more amazingly - picked her up and hugged her saying: "*Thank you so much for marrying me*".
 He was in the New Year's Honours List. He was going to be "Sir George".

The first cloud on the horizon had been at the Christmas just  before they moved to The Manor. It was one of the many Charity Dinners the couple had attended at the London venue Susan called the "Scots Club": he, attracting the sort of attention that only a very rich and successful man can; she, her now-stupendous cleavage attracting the approval of the men and the disapproval of their ladies.

Susan sighed a little as she remembered how she loved her "Scots Club"– the tartans, the music, the girls who sang sad songs in a strange northern  language and the important men and their wives letting their hair down and singing wild songs and using funny guttural words. And despite the fact she was often teased about being English, she felt important too, for the first time in her life - she would be photographed alongside someone who had been on TV the previous night giving an expert opinion on some matter. Not only that – she had met a man who had become Prime Minister! And the Prime Minister seemed to know her husband!

After the food and formalities on that festive occasion, Susan found herself alone at a table when a white-haired old Scot sat down beside her. She was used to such men finding her at such events and busying themselves with trying to show how rich and successful they were also. But on this occasion, her companion, whom she had often noted with a twinkly expression, had no such motive and had a noticeably steely look in his eye when he began:
*"Your husband's from Fife. I am from Stirlingshire where we have a saying: If you shake hands with a man from Fife be sure to count your fingers afterwards."*
Then seeing her bemused expression, he continued: *"Can I ask you if you have any idea about money?"*
*"I know how to spend it"*, she laughed.
*"Aye right enough! But have you heard of a thing called a Ponzi Scheme?"*

*"I know nothing of Finance  - I only know what George always says: If you can't sell to need  then sell to greed and there's a lot of greedy fools out there!"*

*"Aye right enough!"* There was a sigh then the customary twinkle returned. *"I hear you'll have good news in the New Year and - if you'll excuse me - I must awa' and hae a wee word with Mister Macrae yonder."*

The old Scot had thus conducted himself politely but Susan had sensed she had been given some sort of warning.

The knighthood duly arrived in the January and with it came their move to The Manor. But the expected dinner parties did not occur and the invitations to the charity events dried up.  Susan found she was marooned in a gilded cage with a butler and household staff who were polite to her face but clearly knew she had no idea how to run a household and so appeared to do as they chose.

Of course she should have been happy. This was everything she had dreamt of since  a school visit to a "stately home" had planted the seeds of ambition. Now she had all that – except the peacocks on the lawn and she was not really sure she liked peacocks anyway.  But it was an empty world with her husband away most of the time. A world of the swimming pool, watching TV and  - increasingly – the drinks cabinet.

Yes -she should have been happy at The Manor but deep down knew she had never been so unhappy for she knew there was something wrong. Susan had not forgotten the canny old Scot at the Christmas event and remembered the word "Ponzi" which she at first assumed was yet another of the quaint Scottish words which attendees at those events used - particularly after a dram or two. When she asked Carter the butler, if he knew anything about the word,  he replied with his customary suavity: *"I believe it to be some sort of dubious financial device, Madam. Such matters do not normally come to my notice."* On a rare occasion when her husband was at The Manor, she asked him about the word but  was told in no uncertain terms that it was not her province to ask questions on Finance matters. Susan remembered just how hurt she had been with the term by which she had been addressed on that occasion. She thought she was actually very clever in hooking a multi-millionaire.

Then, of course, came the turning point - the time when the "greedy fools" wanted their money back and investigations took place and Regulatory Authorities and then the Fraud Squad went into action. But she understood nothing of this until  The Dreadful Day – the one she would never forget.

It was a Friday morning in Summer of 2008 at The Manor when she was awoken by a forceful ringing of the doorbell and a banging on the front door. For some reason, her usual morning haze was not too bad that day and so she was able to pull on a dressing gown and stagger out to the landing in time to see, down below in the front hall, Carter the butler open the door to two broad shouldered men and hear the words *"Warrant for the arrest ..."*,  watch them burst into her husband's study and then reappear with him firmly in their grip propelling him out of the house. Seconds later she heard the banging of  car doors and a vehicle drive off.

Waiting & wondering, well back from the balustrade and not immediately visible from the hallway below, Susan decided to keep well back and await further events. She had not long to wait until there was a second intrusion and  the horrified Susan looked down on lots of uniformed police pouring into the study, to emerge minutes later carrying a computer and piles of box files and other paperwork. When the scrunching on the gravel outside and the sound of voices had ceased and vehicles had driven off, Carter who had calmly observed the proceedings, closed the front door.

For Susan worse was to come, as Carter, clearly oblivious to her presence above – she was not normally seen before noon -  strode back towards the rear of the house, calling out to the staff in a voice she had never heard him use: *"That's it everybody! The jumped up little Scotch git has had his collar felt - surprise – surprise! Got the little cheating beggar at last! You all know what to do now but one of you had better go and tell Boozy Susie."*

Susan remembered that she had staggered back, trancelike, to her room – they had never shared bedrooms -and collapsed on her bed in sudden flood of tears. Then almost to her surprise she sat up and reached instinctively for the bottle of gin on the bedside table but then rejected it in favour of a glass of water from the carafe on the matching table on the other side of her large luxurious bed. Then she found couple of paracetamol tablets from the bottle which was housed in the drawer below and swigged them down.

The usual respectful knock on the bedroom door was soon to follow with the maid entering expecting to find her mistress in the usual comatose state and very surprised to be curtly dismissed.

Susan would always remember that moment when she realised she was a despised alcoholic married to an equally despised fraudster. She spent a long, long time in the en-suite shower noting sadly that her  assets had slumped in every way. Then she dressed herself in the plainest things she could find in a wardrobe not noted for plain things. She went downstairs, still in a haze and into the Morning Room, suddenly hungry and suddenly noticing a total stillness in the house. She went through into an empty kitchen. Caps and gowns and aprons were neatly folded on the table where also lay, with a mug and plate as paper weights, a number of letters. In the half hour or so since the arrest of Sir George, whilst she had been showering, and dressing, the staff had been busy. Each letter contained the same message of resignation with immediate effect with a note she did not understand about Holiday Pay but with a forwarding address. It was as though they had been expecting this to happen. Even the Gardener's Boy had deserted her!

Then she did two things she had not done in years: digging around in unfamiliar cupboards and drawers, she made herself a breakfast of a bowl of sugary cornflakes and a mug of tea, then she rang her mother.

"Good old Mum!" Parked in the layby, Susan spoke out loud again. Sensible little Mrs. Caldicott who had taken it all in her stride just as she had done with Mr. Caldicott's death a few months earlier.

On the Dreadful Day, Mum braved the M25 and drove all the way round London to The Manor. She helped Susan pack a few necessaries, found instructions for the burglar alarm and  by ringing the suppliers arranged for a security firm to watch over the now empty premises. Then she wheeled Susan south to Purley.

Arrived in the family home, the wonderful little Mrs. Caldicott then coaxed the name of the couple's lawyer out of Susan's befuddled memory and quickly established that bank accounts and credit cards had been frozen and - in effect - Susan had no access to cash. But Dad  - dear  Dad who had worked himself into an early grave and scrimped and saved for a retirement he never saw -had left them very well off – and Mum assured her that she was not to worry about money.

Parked in the layby, Susan had stopped thinking of "chapters" but she liked to organise facts. In fact she had found that what she really liked in life was order BUT an order that she could control. So she began to count on her fingers all the actions her splendid Mum – just "little Mrs Caldicott who works at the newsagents" -had taken  with never a word of censure in the years and months following her flight from The Manor. The nearest Mum had come to upbraiding her about her previous lifestyle was in a quiet moment late one night when she pointed out that Susan was a "trophy" – darkly hinting that it was the boobs not the person George was interested in. That the liaison should become a marriage, Mum had suggested, was merely to improve his chances of getting a knighthood from a Prime Minister who was  a son of the Manse and so probably disapproved of co-habiting couples.


Susan began ticking off the list. Mum had:
Straightway contacted a lawyer friend from her Bridge Club and got divorce proceedings underway; got her into Rehab Clinic; arranged for breast reduction surgery; again through the Bridge Club, arranged driving lessons and, using some of her Dad's legacy money, got her the little car she was in now.

And Mum was at her side during all the Legal Proceedings when she discovered what it was  that her husband did that made them so rich. Listening to the witnesses at the  Trial, she heard and understood for the first time, how he left the Finance  House  where  he  was  so  successful  and  so respected, to set up on his own account. Two of his former colleagues  joined  him  and  they  also  persuaded  a  young Asian man to set up a sparkling website. All three testified that  the  enterprise  was  totally  above  board  to  start  with although there was a high element of risk involved. The early high returns were not sustainable but the cash kept pouring in. At that point, Sir George had then decided to keep paying out at the same rate using  the cash from the new subscribers to his "Wealth Fund"  instead of returns from investments. All three colleagues had been horrified at this turn of events and had resigned, a fact which had not gone un-noticed in the media.  Even then, investors were not  deterred,  presumably  as  a  result  of  the  amazing apparent record of the Fund which seemed to be bucking the trend and the reputation and status of "Golden George" who  had  friends  in  high  places  and  had  become  "Sir George".

Susan  listened  while   the  expensively  hired  Defence Counsel portrayed him as a hapless victim of circumstances now abandoned by friends and colleagues and deserted by his wife. A very convincing picture was painted of a public benefactor worthy of  knighthood who had used his best endeavours to fulfil his promises to his investors rather than one perpetrating a multi-million -pound fraud. Susan was almost convinced and was on the edge of believing she had misjudged her husband until Mum had reminded her how he had described those investors as "greedy fools".

Mum, of course, had been horrified by what she considered to be the very light sentence imposed at the conclusion of the Trial and became very much involved in activities whereby all Sir George's remaining assets  were used to repay at least some money to the investors. But she had continued her active  support of her daughter importantly getting her a position as a volunteer with a charity she worked for. Then the charity helped Susan get onto a training course, then offered her a full-time job, for she had discovered in her new- found sobriety that she had inherited her father's aptitude for figures plus her mother's organising skill and so went from  strength to strength. Then her ex-husband had contacted her, pleading forgiveness and saying he wished to see her.

She had great doubts  - he had always been SO persuasive could she stand up to him?  But her mother persuaded her: *Go and show him who you are now. If he starts wheedling -remember the names he called you.*
"That was that - this is this" she said out loud as she re-started the car engine. "So Susan - let's get on with it." He had asked to see her – not the other way round and he was going to have to realise that the world had changed. *Sorry George but the woman you are about to meet is  not the silly big breasted bimbo of yesteryear. Nor am I the stupid ignorant b**** you once called me.* Remembering the last scene in the last episode of a favourite TV series: "Lovejoy", she borrowed some words. "The past is a different country and Susan Caldicott doesn't live there anymore" she said out loud.

BUT –the nagging doubt remained. Yes, he had called her names  - but so had  lots of people: "Easy Susie" - "Boozy Susie" – were just some. Maybe he had really tried to repay the investors in good faith as his Counsel had said.

 Then came the memory which brought all her earlier resolution flooding back – the memory of the smirk on his face in court when the charges of large- scale fraud were dismissed and all he could be convicted of was "False Accounting" – with  even the maximum sentence less remission  amounting to little more than a few months in an Open Prison. That did it! She eased her own little car out into the traffic stream, Susan Caldicott was back in control. *End of story George – it was YOU that was the greedy fool. GOOD AFTERNOON.*

# AUTHOR'S POSTSCRIPT

As we take leave of the now very determined Susan and hope perhaps that her ex-husband may also be a reformed character who might take up a charity role, there are some references in this tale which some readers would appreciate my clarifying.

In the UK, an **Open Prison** is any jail in which the prisoners are trusted to serve their sentences with minimal supervision and perimeter security and are often not locked up in their prison cells and are only for prisoners considered a low risk to the public.

Our Sir George was indeed running a **Ponzi Scheme**, a form of fraud that lures investors with promises of higher than average returns but actually pays earlier investors with funds from more recent investors in the guise of profits. The scheme's assets and growth strategy remain opaque to the investors and can maintain the illusion of a sustainable operation as long as new and existing investors believe in its advertised credibility. Problems arise when investors begin to ask for a return of their original investments which we may believe to be the case in this Tale.

These schemes have a long history and if you seek further information, *Wikipedia* is very informative. To attract investors, our Sir George would have issued some sort of Prospectus which contained misleading claims as to the nature of his Fund. There is  where the Law would have caught him [Section 17 of the Theft Act 1968] and on his conviction, he would have been liable for imprisonment for up to seven years for the offence of **False Accounting.**

That sentence would have been enough to activate the United Kingdom **Honours Forfeiture Committee** who had clearly in this case decided that our Sir George should no longer be allowed to hold his knighthood and had recommended the Monarch accordingly. Our Tale takes place just as Her Majesty was rescinding the honour.

**Lovejoy** for those not acquainted, is a British television comedy-drama mystery series, adapted by Ian La Frenais from the picaresque novels by John Grant , writing under the pen name Jonathan Gash. The show, concerning the adventures of a roguish antiques dealer, which ran to 71 episodes over six series, was originally broadcast on BBC1 between January 1986 and December 1994 and has been often repeated. Co-incidentally, by way of explaining the five-year gap between the first and second series, the title character is seen as serving a sentence in an Open Prison.

Apologies from someone with Stirlingshire roots to the worthy folk of the Kingdom of Fife.

# JULY 1940

"Good afternoon, Sir George."

"Ah, Bill, you've found me," said Sir George Welland, rising from his table to greet his visitor with a handshake. "I was beginning to think I had made a mistake about which Lyons' Corner House you wanted us to meet in. I'm not very familiar with these places."

"No more am I," replied the other as the two sat down. "But I thought The Strand would be convenient for you and that we would be unlikely to be seen here by anyone who knows us."

"I wouldn't be too sure of that! There's a lot of strange people about these days! But the location is indeed a very handy one for me. And of course – with the threat of bombing there aren't a lot of people around. Now let's try to get the attention of  one of these – what d'you call 'em - 'Nippies'."

The uniformed waitress duly attended and Sir George, awkward in an unfamiliar venue, ordered as his wife had suggested, a pot of tea for two and two toasted teacakes, commenting: "My wife tells me there is no diminution from the pre-war standard."

 Sir George had passed Lyons' Corner House in the Strand many times without being tempted to enter although his wife had spoken favourably of the quality of the tea and of the service. That, of course, had been before the outbreak of war and by, this first week of July 1940, life had changed. However, there was nothing particularly new about senior managers from competing aircraft manufacturers meeting clandestinely but Sir George, now given a major position with the Air Ministry, was no longer in that role. Thus, when

Bill had rung him out of the blue to suggest a meeting without specifying a reason, he had come to a private conclusion as to what the subject matter might be. With that supposition in mind, he was not particularly looking forward to the occasion and decided not to beat about the bush.

"Bill, it is good to see you and, of course, always a pleasure to meet but I fear I may be going to disappoint you."

"We shall see", replied his visitor. " But .. I know you have the ear of Beaverbrook."

"There are other parts of that man's anatomy I would like to have. You know he was insufferably rude to Wilfrid Freeman?"

"It is matter of common knowledge. In fact, it is relevant to what I want to talk to you about."


"Look - if this is about jet propulsion then .."

"Not at all!"

"You surprise me!" replied Sir George, meaning it. "I had heard you had opened a rather  secretive plant somewhere. I assumed you were off on some unofficial jet propulsion project – which I could not possibly back given where we are at present."

Bill broke into a smile.

"You're on the wrong tack, old man – we are developing a fast, twin- engined bomber – one that's mainly constructed from wood. We don't need to wait for your jet engines because these new Merlins will do the job. And we MAKE them!"

"Ahhh! Wood again! That old thing!"

"Hear me out! I know you chaps are for all metal construction and it has benefits but so does our idea –

remember we would not be encroaching on existing plant and current metal aircraft production."

"Point taken but where do I come in?"

Bill pursed his lips and frowned.

"Beaverbrook has forbidden us to make new aircraft."

"Good Lord – did he put it in writing?"

" Not that I know, but he is clear that our role is to use existing plant to make training aircraft, repair fighters, and manufacture Merlin engines under licence. We can do better than that!"

"I have dealt with this man", said Sir George firmly. "It is my belief that by now, Beaverbrook will have forgotten about restricting your output! Anyway you appear to have gone ahead irrespective."

"We have! We have set up a separate plant so technically we're not in breach of any agreement to use existing plant!"

"And I thought you were going behind my back with some jet- propelled job! Presumably, your project is well advanced?"

"Yes in terms of design. We will have an aircraft with a wooden fuselage and skin. There's no rivets with wood so you have an air-smooth surface and we get a fast lightweight fighter bomber."

"Then you will have done something this country didn't manage in the last war."

"Exactly", agreed Bill, happily sensing the conversation was going his way. "But we need your help to overcome the Beaver who was dead set against the idea when Freeman suggested it ages ago. In fact he was very rude about it. There is no time to lose."

The arrival of the "Nippy" with their order gave both men time to pause for thought as they turned the attention to the tea and toasted teacakes.

"These tea cakes really are excellent – I must tell the wife", commented Sir George.

Bill, with his mouth full, nodded assent.

His companion had made up his mind.

"I'm sorry Bill but I can't go to Beaverbrook directly. That would just complicate matters. But I know the man. He only talks to top men so  I think we know who has to  do the job?"

"I think we can find the man at Hatfield."

Sir George began ticking off points with his right index finger on the outstretched fingers of his left hand.

"One: tell Beaverbrook you've a well-developed plan for fast twin- engined bomber. Don't go on about those fast civilian aircraft you made before the War. He's a newspaper man and that's yesterday's news. With me?"

"Certainly!"

"Two: Don't say wood, say composite but the large use of wood means no drawing on the metal needed for Spits etc. The Beaver will like that."

"Good point"

"Three: The fellow is obsessed with speed of production so get your head man to promise, say, 50 by Dec 1941. That's probably impossible but he's not in our industry and doesn't know that."

"Cunning!"

"Four: your clincher - tell Beaverbrook that you have a very fast light bomber which can strike Luftwaffe bases and being as fast as a fighter, can escape pursuit. Make what you are saying sound like newspaper headlines – the man's basically a newsman - if you are giving him a headline like BRITISH BOMBER FLIES FASTER THAN NAZI FIGHTERS – he'll love it. Freeman would have been  far too gentlemanly."

"You're a strategist George."

"Right-oh then! Just an afterthought so I know we've got it right. You are going to use a lot wood which is fine – we have a lot of that but – you of all people MUST know this! – any construction using wood requires considerable skill. The major construction skills in this country are the skills of the railway industry and there is not a lot of wood in a locomotive – sorry – I'm playing Devil's Advocate. "

"What do they make in High Wycombe?"

"If memory serves me  - furniture."

"Out of?"

"Wood – of course. I see what you mean -you do have a skill base to draw on."

 "And in keeping with current practice – we could build components on various sites and assemble aircraft wherever. You do not need large factories which would be targets for the Luftwaffe -at a push groups of neighbours could make bits in  a garden shed. "

"My goodness me! You have thought this through! British aircraft building transformed into a cottage industry. Don't tell The Beaver that – he'll think you're mad!"

"Maybe not, he does believe in dispersing factories because we seem likely to face a bombing onslaught prior to an attempted invasion."

"That is, of course , in the forefront of everybody's minds." Sir George gave a cautious look about him and having decided no one was in earshot, continued: " Bill, strictly in confidence, I tell you what I have told the powers-that-be, for what it's worth."

"Coming from you – I'm sure it's worth a lot," averred Bill firmly.

"Then this is my appraisal," Sir George resumed firmly.

"Our immediate job is to STALL Germany. Hitler will certainly try to attack us, first with an aerial onslaught. I think that is imminent. I firmly believe that these new fighters will be a match for his bomber fleet and the Spitfire can match his Messerschmitt. Crossing the Channel and landing an Army on English shores has never been an easy task. These days, without air cover, I believe it to be impossible. So we will then enter some sort of stalemate. What you are planning and what I am planning will help us fight back. We can't defeat this new German Empire on our own even with our own Navy and Imperial strength. We will need the Americans somehow, sometime. This is what Winston has been saying. We will have to hope that Hitler or an ally of his does something silly and annoys them. In the meantime we have to be seen to be fighting and producing world-class fighting machines and that means aircraft."

The two parted out on The Strand, Sir George who had insisted on paying for the snack, saying cheerfully:
"Bill you may not realise it but you've made my day!"
"Likewise, George. The next part of the War Effort starts right now."

As he walked back along the Strand to the Air Ministry building in Aldwych, Sir George took stock mentally. He had righted a wrong done to the admirable Wilfrid Freeman, he was about to put one over on Beaverbrook and he felt sure he had pointed Bill's firm in the direction of producing a war winning weapon. On the whole, it had been  A GOOD AFTERNOON

# AUTHOR'S POSTSCRIPT

The savvy reader will have spotted that we are here talking about the genesis of a remarkable Second World War aircraft, the De Havilland DH 98 Mosquito. Today, an aircraft which could perform equally well as fighter, bomber or fighter-bomber would be given the terminology which Graham M Simons recognises in the title of his definitive study: *Mosquito: The Original Multi-Role Combat Aircraft.* [I consulted the Pen & Sword 2015 edition.] The twin- engined aircraft, primarily of wooden construction, surpassed its designers' expectations but its design nearly never "got off the drawing board". That the prototype took to the air in November 1940 and mass production began in July 1941 must have been due to a change a heart by Beaverbrook in circumstances which may not have been too far from those suggested in this wholly fictional account. History tells us that Mosquito parts were indeed manufactured by small groups in garden sheds!

Simons tells us its wooden construction led to its being nicknamed "The Flying Tea Chest" but we youngsters came to know it as "The Wooden Wonder" – for indeed it was!

I apologise to those who may be concerned if Beaverbrook [William Maxwell Aitken, 1st Baron Beaverbrook, (1879 – 1964)], is herein portrayed in an unfavourable light. So I must acknowledge that he played a major role in mobilising industrial resources as Winston Churchill's Minister of Aircraft Production. He was a Canadian-British newspaper publisher and backstage politician who was an influential figure in British media and politics of the first half of the 20th century. His base of power was the largest circulation newspaper in the world, the *Daily Express*, which appealed to the conservative working class with intensely patriotic news and editorials.  He is a character who has had his admirers and detractors. Our "Sir George Welland" [See Chapter II in the first of this little series :*Good Morning, Sir George*] would appear to be in the latter camp.

The chosen location of this tale is one of the many establishments of J. Lyons & Co. "Joe Lyons" were best known for their chain of tea shops which opened from 1894 and finally closed in 1981, and for the Lyons' Corner Houses in the West End of London. Our venue is one of those: the  Strand Corner House at the junction of Strand (south side) and Craven Street. Opened 1915, it closed 1977 and the site is now "re-developed" .Service to the table was by uniformed waitresses with the corporate brand  *Nippies,* who disappeared after the War when the tea shops converted to cafeteria service.

"Bill" is a wholly fictional concept, a composite of the talented De Havilland design team but the Wilfrid Freeman referred to is Air Chief Marshal Sir Wilfrid Rhodes Freeman, (1888 –1953). Without question, this man was one of the most important influences on the rearmament of the RAF in the years up to and including the Second World War. As Air Member for Research and Development from 1936, Freeman can be seen to be responsible for the RAF acquiring its Spitfires and Hurricanes and also its Halifax and Lancaster bombers. He played an equally vital role later in the development of the Merlin-engined P-51 Mustang.

 If this Tiny Tale has done nothing else, I hope it will serve as paying homage to Freeman, a man who with some justification may be called a "war winner".

# MAY 1944

"Good Afternoon, Sir George."

Advancing to the red-shawled lady seated with her typewriter on a table on the veranda of the Buckinghamshire dwelling, Sir George found he was unable to find the correct manner of address to respond to her welcome, so he avoided trying.

"It is indeed a good afternoon, the first for some time. Your maid said you were working out here and that you might be taking a short break so I do apologise for disturbing you. I promise I will not take more than a moment of your time."

"Not at all, Sir George, you are very welcome to Green Hedges and indeed I was having my customary midday break. I had no idea we had such a distinguished neighbour."

"I am not sure I count as distinguished."

"You are too modest, Sir George. I am told by Cook that you have made a great contribution to the War effort and that you are up there with Beaverbrook and Churchill."

" I cannot imagine where those tales have come from," smiled Sir George.  "However, my contribution to the nation's efforts is having a rest for a few days, hence I was happy to undertake a small domestic errand. Though Dinah and Lucy Ann, my granddaughters, had made me aware that their favourite author lived close by, I had not realised until this morning that that it was to her household that we were coming to the rescue."

"And Cook and my maid – who seem to be in close contact with your own staff - let me know that it would be you in person who would deliver this vital ingredient. I must say, it is terribly good of your wife to help."

"No problem at all . We inherited my wife's late aunt's kitchen – more valuable than cash these days! – which meant that we doubled up in some cases. The vanilla essence was one example. It is pre-war no doubt but I am sure it will fill the gap that so troubles your cook."
"I don't think I have met your wife."
"I believe not. She is, of course, very busy with all the worthy activities she threw herself into since we moved out of London."
Sir George was very conscious of temporising. The fact was that his wife, who had a low opinion of "creative types" to start with, had no wish to meet one who, even worse, was a woman who had divorced and almost immediately re-married. His wife's opinions were, however, of no consequence in the present conversation and he thrust the recollection to the back of his mind as his host continued in her pleasant manner.
"We moved here from Bourne End before the War. We had a lovely cottage there but we needed a bigger house and we felt we needed to be closer to London. Have you been here long?"
"We moved after the War had begun. We were rather pressurised by the Powers That Be or the Powers That Were  at that time to move away from central London."
"During the Blitz?"
"Before that actually. It was suggested we move to somewhere that was unlikely to be a target for the Luftwaffe but still fairly easily reachable by train from London."
"Yes we have been spared the agonies which I understand our cities suffered. Although – as you will recall – there were some scares and we did have to go to our shelter."
"Indeed yes. I see, that like most of us, you have an Anderson Shelter."

"My daughters called it our 'bunny burrow'!"

"They do rather alter the look of a garden."

"The War has done that in every respect. Ours, as you see, is much given to the Dig For Victory campaign. My husband and I had to do most of the work ourselves. We often worked until late at night."

"We had always lived in central London so when we came here I was amazed how my wife took  to gardening. It appears she has hitherto unsuspected "green fingers". She is a  great fan of Mr Middleton's gardening programme on the wireless."

"So are we. Have you had evacuees billeted on you?"

"Due to the hush-hush nature of a lot of my work, we were exempt. Have you had any?"

"I have staff and their  family living here so technically the house is full This war is so dreadful. Everything has been disrupted. Have you managed any holidays?"

"We had hoped to go down to Cornwall as we have managed to do throughout  but there's a big show coming off shortly and my boy Jack seems rather busy and, anyway, I assume civilian travel will continue to be restricted. We do love Cornwall in the spring and early summer. There's a family house we go to – on the north coast by a small peninsula called Pedngarrow."

" I do love those Cornish names!"

 "Yes indeed. The house was a mine manager's we think. It's up on a hill called Carn Garrow which – I think - translates as 'craggy tops'."

"What a wonderful name – 'Craggy Tops'!"

"I suppose the area has a rather romantic tinge. There is a rocky little islet just offshore. There was one year we arrived at Carn Garrow and there was a sea fret and the islet looked most mysterious. Dinah and Lucy Ann concocted a wonderful story about there being a secret passage to the island from our house used by smugglers!”

“What imaginative granddaughters you have, Sir George!”

“And they are huge fans or your work and regular readers of *Sunny Stories* magazine. And now I must admit an ulterior motive behind this visit. When they learnt we had your good self as a near neighbour they prevailed upon me to get your signature in their Autograph Books and they will be with us next week.  Hence my air of urgency. I have the books with me.”

 Sir George produced from his jacket pocket two small, decorated notebooks. “Can I presume upon you?”

“Of course”, smiled his hostess. “Their names again?”

* * * * *

Mightily relieved that  he had, at last, fulfilled his promise to his  wife and family, Sir George strolled  homeward past the suburban hedges.  The divorcee did not strike him as being the louche character his wife seemed to suggest. Additionally, he had successfully sidestepped the problem of how to address his lady host and avoided a *faux pas.* So he could count it a GOOD AFTERNOON.

# AUTHOR'S POSTSCRIPT

The savvy reader will have quickly spotted that the lady author in the Tale, the resident of the now vanished 8 - bedroom Mock-Tudor detached house, *Green Hedges,* in Beaconsfield, Bucks., is none other than Enid Blyton [1897 – 1968]. That she is the subject of this tale arises out of my wholehearted respect for anyone who could, as a matter of daily routine, write between 6,000 and 10,000 words between breakfast and tea!

 Apologies to members of Enid Blyton Society for trespassing on their patch and hope they will excuse my boldness as have those of The Arthur Ransome Society after reading *Good Morning, Sir George.* My source was the admirable *ENID BLYTON: the BIOGRAPHY*; Barbara Stoney [Tempus Publishing 2006 edition.]

The **Anderson shelter** was NOT named after its inventor but from Sir John Anderson, the UK Cabinet Minister who had special responsibility for preparing air-raid precautions immediately prior to the outbreak of the Second World War It would seem a  reasonable enough choice of naming as it was he who  initiated the development of the shelter.

The shelters comprised sheets of galvanised corrugated steel panels put together in a kit capable of self-assembly by a householder. I can well remember Dad engaged in the toil of digging out the 4ft [1.2m] deep trench in our garden to accommodate the structure. At 6 feet (1.8 m) high, 4.5 feet (1.4 m) wide, and 6.5 feet (2.0 m) long the shelters were designed to accommodate up to six adults. The excavated soil was used to cover the shelter and the planting of this with flowers and vegetables together with the construction of steps down to the entrance became a matter of pride for many households. One would assume that it was so at *Green Hedges.*


**Dig For Victory** was a Government wartime campaign to maximise use of land to grow vegetable crops. A feature was the gardening broadcasts given on BBC radio by "**Mr Middleton**" [ Cecil Henry Middleton (1886 – 1945)]. He was a Gardening writer, one of the earliest radio and television broadcasters on gardening for the BBC, whose good-humoured and informative short talks could command an audience of over three million.


It seems possible that the prolific author drew upon her subconscious memory for the characters and locations portrayed in her works. So let us note that *Island of Adventure,* one of the very first books this unprolific writer ever owned , was published in the November of the year of our Tale where the names Jack,  Dinah and Lucy-Ann appear in a setting of a coastal house called Craggy Tops.

# FEBRUARY 1946

*Unusually for these Tales there is an* AUTHOR'S PREFACE. *Readers may have quite recently found themselves in a world where the Government directed their lives with a seemingly endless stream of restrictions. This Tale is of a time before central heating had become commonplace when – would you believe – not everybody had a telephone and the Government was involved in every facet of life  - in particular, what you could eat.*

"Good Afternoon, Sir George."

The greeting was in unison from the two ladies, clearly in their Sunday best, but keeping their coats on, who had been shown into the Drawing Room of the Hall where Sir George had been standing by the window watching their arrival. He had deemed it impolite to have them shown into the Library which, during this flying visit to the ancestral home, had become his untidily cluttered den but was undoubtedly warmer. He was beginning to regret his decision.

His guests were both younger than he had imagined after receiving an extremely well-written letter from a  Mrs. Anne C. Yule, of Stockton Heath, Warrington,  who had latter telephoned for an appointment as he had suggested when he replied by return.

All in all, he was beginning to feel embarrassed about the arrangements he had made for what would the first visitors to the Hall for a very long time.  Perhaps he should have mentioned that the fine old building had still not been properly re-opened after the War and that he was merely on a short trip up from his London base. Perhaps it would have sounded as though he were putting them off if he had explained that the only staff were Perks, the aging general factotum who lived in the Lodge and Mrs. Peaker, the wife of one of his tenant farmers, who had agreed to double as housekeeper over the few days he was spending there. But it was such a well-constructed letter that had asked for his help and Mrs. Yule had been so well spoken on the telephone he really felt he had to agree to meet.

Standing in the window, memories came flooding back. First, of a party in that same room, his only son, at the centre of the jollity, looking so smart in his RAF uniform and so proud of his pilot's wings. And then of the telegram, eighteen months after that which carried the news that meant the self-same happy young man would never return and consequently his mother could not now bear to be in the Hall.

He had watched as the Hillman Minx had pulled up on the gravel drive, the sonorous tones of the Harrison long case clock in the hall chiming three o'clock and witnessing their promptness. He had heard Perks, in his butler role, admit them and hear them politely decline his offer to take their coats – much needed in the Cheshire mid-winter chill - before ushering in the pair and announce in tones rarely used in recent times: *Mrs Yule and Mrs Nairn, Sir George.* Aware that the elegant room, under dust covers until that morning, was chill and unwelcoming and, hoping to overcome that, he switched on his best smile and turned in greeting.

"Good Afternoon, ladies. Welcome to the Hall. Please come and sit down by the fire. Thank you, Perks. Please ask Mrs Peaker to bring in the afternoon tea. Ladies, I have taken the liberty of ordering tea for you though I am afraid that the current rationing situation rather limits our hospitality and the lack of fuel has meant this is a rather poor fire, I'm afraid."

*[When asked later about their visit, the ladies were to describe The Hall as: "Old and cold"]*

Once more wishing that he had arranged to meet in the Library, for despite its unkempt condition, the fire there kept it warm. Here, the stuttering fire – a poor effort compared to its surroundings  - did little to dissipate the chill of the expensively upholstered room and Sir George felt he had to muster all his charm.

"You found your way to the Hall without too much trouble, I trust? " he enquired.

Perching herself rather nervously on the edge of one of the settees, Anne replied: "My husband and I had a trial run on Sunday afternoon – these Cheshire lanes are terribly confusing - the signposts haven't all been put back after the War."

"I have spoken to the County Council – they are still in store but there is so much to do and there's the manpower shortage everywhere.."

"We were lucky!" Anne continued. "Mrs. Nairn's neighbour found a map in an old book. They didn't know they'd got it, otherwise it would have been handed in at the start of the War with all the rest. We managed to navigate using that."

"Mrs. Yule is a very good driver," said Betty Nairn firmly, sensing – quite incorrectly - that Sir George was questioning her friend's confidence and competence. "She's been driving for years. She delivered the groceries for her father all over Stirlingshire. And she drove in West Africa!"

"You are probably more competent than I am, Mrs. Yule," laughed Sir George. "You have a Hillman Minx, I see. A good car, I am told."

"Yes, we bought it in South Wales just before the War. It has only got a six- volt battery so the windscreen wipers aren't very good. I'm glad that awful rainy spell is over .."

"That was just terrible", interrupted Betty. "Mind you that wind is awfy cold the day."

Anne continued her story of the family car: "We're so glad to have it back after the War when it was laid up at my parents' in Scotland. We can't do much motoring with this petrol rationing but it will do thirty miles to the gallon."

A rattle of crockery and a knock on the door heralded the entrance of Mrs Peaker and an end to the conversational trivia.

To the disappointment of both ladies who had hoped perhaps for some touch of pre-war luxury in an aristocratic household, the fare was meagre. *"Just one puir wee scone apiece",* Betty was later to remark.

There was a pause in the flow of conversation as Sir George observed the niceties of the occasion. Then when he deemed the moment right, moved to the business of the afternoon.

"At the outset, ladies", he said in his Chairman-of-the-Board voice. "Can we please make this clear – neither of you are connected with any political party or with this new British Housewives' League and you are not here as delegates of any sort. Am I right?"

Slightly surprised, as she had made no mention of any such connection in her letter or subsequent phone call, Anne replied: "Do you know Warrington?"

"I'm afraid I don't really know Warrington at all", stated Sir George apologetically. "My family have always banked

there  - Warrington does have a reputation for shall we say
– financial prudence. But I have little cause to go into the
town - even for the train, as there is a little local station.
Actually, I spend most of my life in London – my wife much
prefers life there – I'm only up here to attend to some estate
management business after the floods in Northwich. But
that splendid clock in the hall was made in Warrington by
a John Harrison - and Perks - very much a Warrington
man  - tells me he was a very famous clockmaker."
Anne continued: "We are both members of the same
Church ..."
Betty's strident Ayrshire tones interrupted: "And there's
three of us really. My sister Margaret is staying back so she
can take care of our laddies after the school."
"Yes", continued Anne. "We're all from St John's
Presbyterian Church on Wilderspool Causeway in
Warrington."
"They all call it the Scots church", added Betty.
"I can understand why", laughed Sir George. "You are
clearly  both Scots. I assume you came down in with your
husbands in the War."
"Yes indeed", replied Anne. "Bob is a civil engineer and he
was involved in the construction of all those military bases
round Warrington – though we were over in Northern
Ireland too."
Ever one to move progress, Betty explained: "It was
Margaret and me who wanted Mrs. Yule to write to
someone. And Mrs. Yule's father suggested you."
"It was an excellent letter Mrs Yule," commented Sir
George, hoping that he did not sound too condescending
"You are clearly an experienced correspondent."
"I am used to writing letters and I was in the Civil Service
before I got married but it is kind of you to say so and it was

indeed  my father who suggested I write and try to meet you."

This rather puzzled Sir George. "Your father? In Scotland?"

" Yes. He keeps a grocery business in Stirlingshire and so he is very close to the day-to-day problems of all this rationing and he knows the Grocery Trade well, as his father ran the shop before him. He saw your name in an article in the trade magazine. It mentioned you lived here at the Hall and so Father thought you might be able to meet and hear what we housewives are thinking. He put that in the weekly letter I get from home. Hence my letter to you."

" Aha! Like me, the Grocery Trade is in the family!" The picture was becoming clear to Sir George.

Anne came to the point and in an indignant tone began: "It's this business of the Dried Egg Powder being withdrawn. We can't get fresh  eggs and we're used to that but .. but .."

A forceful Betty decided to drive home the point. "We all knew that rationing was important during the War but this is just terrible – taking away our Dried Egg! It's very good and we can cook and bake with it so we can just about manage with having only one fresh egg each a week and making that our Sunday breakfast."

At last Sir George found himself on firm ground and knew he could speak authoritatively. "Well Mrs  Yule, your Father is correct. I am, with a number of leaders of industry – including the food wholesale and retail trades – currently pressurising the Government.  In particular we're after this fella Smith – this ex-cabby – to reverse that wrong decision on Dried Egg Powder. Be assured, ladies, the matter *IS* in hand!"

The ladies had no desire to prolong their stay in the cold, dank Drawing Room and spotted their chance to leave.

"We have to get back", said Betty. "We 've our family to see to. Our boys, Robert and Donald will go straight from the school to my sister Margaret's. We arranged for them to have tea with her boys."

"We'll pick up my daughter, Esther", added Anne. "She's three in July. She's at my neighbours - where I went to telephone you  - they're good at looking after her and we'll all meet up. I said to expect us when they see us but .."

"Of course", said Sir George and pulled a cord which rang a bell which summoned Perks.

The satisfied ladies stood and Sir George rather awkwardly shook hands with both.

"You have clearly gone to some trouble ladies but I as I said I think you will find that the supply problems of Dried Egg Powder will be solved shortly. So I think you can take good news back to your families in Warrington."

"The ladies are leaving", said Sir George to Perks, almost unnecessarily as all three were moving out into the Hallway. There, they found a waiting  Mrs Peaker who pressed a brown paper bag into Anne's hands with a quiet word.


So, back in the Hillman - which behaved itself by starting first time in front of an audience of Sir George, Perks and Mrs Peaker -- and with Betty lighting the cigarette she had been gasping for - both women agreed they had been made welcome and had been given good news.

"Nice of them to wave us off", said Anne.

"What was in the bag yon housekeeper body gave you?"

"You never believe it!" said Anne with a twinkle of the eyes.

"Half a dozen eggs! They keep hens. Two for you, two for

Margaret Two for Bobby and me – it'll  be like pre-war again!"

Having bid farewell to his two guests, Sir George returned to the Drawing Room and its inadequate fire and stood with his back to the fireplace deep in thought. Had he been right to suggest that matters were going to improve? He felt sure that he and his friends could put sufficient pressure on the Food Minister to reverse the unnecessary withdrawal of the popular Dried Egg Powder ... *but* .. there was something he had not said: It was possible that bread might have to be to be rationed within the next few months. Should he have mentioned that? The two ladies had made difficult family arrangements, had found their way on un-signposted roads, using up the valuable petrol ration. And  it had not occurred to him, when he wrote inviting her to telephone him, that Mrs Yule might  not have a telephone and needed to go to a neighbour in order to ring him. Surely it was right that he had given them some hope.

 For the first time he had met and spoken directly two ordinary British Housewives who had no obvious political axe to grind and were clearly not involved with the evolving pressure groups of aggrieved housewives. He could meet up with his fellows back in London and speak with real authority as having heard an authentic voice. And Mrs. Peaker had made good the promise she had made that morning to give the visitors something to remember the Hall by. Half a dozen precious fresh eggs!

Suddenly feeling cheered despite the winter gloom, he stepped over to the fireplace and, warming his hands on the still stuttering fire, he told himself that – all in all – it had been a GOOD AFTERNOON.

# AUTHOR'S POSTSCRIPT

Having written a Family Memoir, I make no excuses about bringing my Mum , Mrs Anne Yule [1912-2002] and her friends from Stockton Heath days, Mrs Betty Nairn & Mrs Margaret Lawrence, into this tale of a time of real austerity. I have no illustration of the three but the accompanying image from the Yule Family Album pictures the 1939 Hillman Minx car which features in this otherwise fictional Tale.

This writer well remembers asking for a *"Dried Egg omelette for tea"* so the withdrawal of that popular product certainly caused an uproar.

Regarding the Grandfather or Longcase clock: Sir George & his butler were both mistaken about Harrisons of Warrington. Bill Cooke's discursive *The Story of Warrington: The Athens of the North* [Matador 2020] states conclusively, in Chapter 9, that the John Harrison, clockmaker of Warrington, was NOT the John Harrison of *Longitude* fame. Incidentally, the same work [p265] suggests the origin of Warrington's reputation in financial matters to which Sir George refers, may have arisen from the fact that Parr's Bank, [founded in 1788] whose HQ was in the town until 1890, survived the financial crises in 1797 and 1810 and when many similar  came to grief.

Sir George  was, however, right about Bread Rationing, which was introduced, amidst howls of protest from the public, on 21st July 1946.

Dried Egg Powder, a staple substitute during the Rationing of the 1940's, is also called Powdered Egg. It consists of  fully dehydrated eggs produced using spray drying in the same way that powdered milk is made. As Betty suggested in our Tale, Dried Egg Powder can be used without rehydration when baking and can be rehydrated to make dishes such as scrambled eggs and omelettes. As our Sir George hinted, stocks were soon restored but there began an unprecedented militancy amongst the country's housewives.

Ben Smith [1879 -1964],Trades Unionist and Labour MP, eventually Sir Benjamin Smith,  is  a rather forgotten figure of post-war UK. A driver of one of London's earliest taxicabs, Smith became the first organiser for the London Cab Drivers' Union. He was national organiser of the Transport and General Workers' Union from its formation in 1922 until he was elected to Parliament in 1923 as MP for Rotherhithe. His tenure as  Minister of Food in the 1945 Attlee ministry did not last long after the time of our Tale as he resigned in May 1946. However he continued to do well for himself as he  became the Chairman of West Midlands Coal Board.

 Those seeking more information about that trying time for UK are directed to that excellent tome: *Austerity Britain 1945-51* ;David Kynaston; [Bloomsbury 2007.]

# SEPTEMBER 2015

"Good afternoon, Sir George"

"Good afternoon, Corporal Tyldesley", replied Sir George, almost gasping in the change of appearance in the non-com who had driven him from the station on the previous afternoon. Gone  was the standard service dress of the British Army with the distinctive pullover and belt. Today it was a pleated skirt with a matching bolero top over a crisp white, short-sleeved blouse which revealed  a pair of rather muscular arms. Instead of the beret and hair tied tightly in a bun, the hair now hung attractively over the shoulders and even Sir George could see that a great deal of attention had been paid to her make-up. Her calf-length skirt and her footwear clearly indicated to Sir George's practised eye that she bore no lower limb prostheses though he felt sure he had detected a limp on the previous day,

She was standing in the corridor outside the door of his Guest Room in the MOD Special Facility Rehabilitation Unit in the west of England to which location the Corporal had driven him on the previous afternoon when she collected him off the Paddington train.

"You've come to drive me down to Combe Tallow House then," he continued.

"I'm not too early, am I  sir?"

"Not at all and it's good to see you again. I take it you are off duty?"

"Yessir. This is the afternoon when I usually go down to Combe Tallow."

From just a brief acquaintance from the journey of the previous day, Sir George had decided that he rather liked Corporal Tyldesley. The directness of her speech and brisk manner suggested she was the sort of "can-do" person he admired although he drew the line at addressing her – as she had suggested – as "Tyd".

"I had dinner with Colonel Borthwick last night and I understand you have been a regular visitor to Combe Tallow House", he said , conversationally.

" Indeed yes, Sir George. Lady Janet and Mrs W have been very kind to me."

"Then let us be on our way – I have never been there though my wife and I did get invitations after Harry inherited the place."

Sir George collected a few things and then followed his driver out to the waiting vehicle.  He remained puzzled over the Tyldesley case as she presented no sign of anything other than natural limbs. What was her role here? He had assumed she was a patient in re-hab. He was no expert on British army insignia but her uniform on the previous day had suggested she was an infantry soldier and not a member of the administrative or medical staff. Then he recalled the suggestion made by Borthwick over a very acceptable pub meal the previous evening, that there were worries about her mental state.

"*Not my area*" he told himself, mentally preparing himself for the next few hours. Not only had he to adjust to his driver's northern speech cadences and contralto pitch  but also to a complete change of scene. He was moving from the military rehabilitation unit which had so impressed him, to meeting a lady with whom relations had always seemed difficult.

The soldier was in conversational mode as they walked out of the building.

" I understand from Lady Janet that you and  Sir Henry go back a long way", she began and by way of explanation continued: "She did mention to me she was getting a visit."
"I knew them both back in our student days. "
"That's some time then!"
"Indeed but it's been little more than just Christmas cards over the years and Harry's death came as a bit of a shock. Wish now I'd kept more in touch."

Sir George settled into a  rear seat, not of a  staff car this time but a smaller saloon vehicle which he assumed must be Tyd's own vehicle. Up to now, all had been very gratifying and he felt pleased that he had taken up the invitation to visit made very cordially by Colonel Borthwick, the Unit Director when they had met after the Memorial Service for Sir Henry in London. So pressing indeed had the Director's invitation been that he could hardly forebear to promise to add a visit  to the ever- expanding list of "to do" things before his impending retirement from his Consultant Role – a list that was being managed by Susan, his wife, with her customary  efficiency. And it was at Susan's insistence that he had subsequently found himself engaged in a telephone conversation – not a type of communication he excelled in – with the Colonel.

 After his usual awkwardness in such conversations, he got into his theme that he was  now running things down a bit so had time to finally take up the very kind invitation – not wearing his Consultant's hat of course –but just an informal look around. He received an enthusiastic response from Colonel Borthwick:
*- you'd be very welcome – we have a VIP visitors suite here which should suit you.*

*- Not sure if I deserve VIP status!*

*- A someone who has been at the forefront of the development of prosthetic limbs for years – I think you deserve that in our eyes! Will you be driving?*

*- No - we are rather between vehicles at present – all part of the great retirement plan which my wife is supervising. and what suits in London wouldn't do us in our new place down in Devon.*

*- No matter, we can pick you up, we have plenty of people here who need to re discover their driving skills – let's figure out a couple of nights for you to stay.*

Thus the trip was arranged but subsequently  Lady Susan reminded him that Combe Tallow House was quite close to the Unit. Maybe he could call in on Lady Janet as they hadn't seen her since the Memorial Service in London for his friend from student days.

There followed a more than usually  awkward call to Lady Janet whom Sir George had always thought of, in a dismissive way, as someone who could not tell port from starboard. However, she sounded kindness itself on the phone and was sure the Unit would drive him down and anyway she had a memento for him.

Thus was Sir George put to struggling with a second call to the Unit, stumbling staccato-wise as usual  through his interchange with Colonel Borthwick:

*– inland geography not as good as my coastal –I hadn't realised you are quite close to Harry – Sir Henry's old place at Combe Tallow House – Susan  -my wife thought it would be a good idea if I dropped in there while I was in the area – out of good manners – so to speak.*

*- yes it's close by and we are in contact – Lady Janet has been very helpful and we will miss her when she moves.*
*- I wasn't aware of that!*
*- Apparently the daughter – you may remember her at the Memorial Service -*
*- very different from her mother -*
*-Indeed! Rather affected in speech and manner should we say – well, she and her husband and family will take up residence   when Lady J moves to be with her sister somewhere on the Sussex coast.*
*- then my visit is well timed!*
*- and there will be no problem here running you over to Combe Tallow on that second afternoon. We have plenty of people here who are keen to drive and Mrs W the housekeeper there makes amazing scones so you will do OK.*

The car drew up outside the substantial residence in its own grounds which Sir George's friend from student days had inherited along with the baronetcy. The impressive front door  opened and two ladies emerged, a tweed-dressed one he recognised as Lady Janet and the other, broad-hipped, grey- haired and aproned whom he surmised was Mrs W – the acclaimed scone baker. Sir George was also aware there was a smile on the face of the latter which rather contrasted to the expression on her employer's face. It soon transpired that the smile was for his driver for, with a "Come you round the back with me, my dear", Mrs W had swept Tyd away leaving an awkward Sir George, who was carrying a carefully wrapped small present, with his hostess. [His wife had identified a suitable present to be a decorated plate from the Channel Isles, picked up on a recent yachting expedition.] It was handed over awkwardly and equally awkwardly received.

The pair moved into the spacious and expensively furnished drawing room where a table had been prepared with - as heralded - a plate of freshly buttered scones. Sir George took the proffered seat and began to partake of the tea and scones which, he was able to relate later, were of outstanding quality. Then, when it seemed to be the polite moment he turned his attention to a sealed envelope on the table which was marked "SPECIAL - KEEP FOR GEORGE".

"The memento I presume?"

"Yes please take it. Harry kept just about every scorecard of every match he went to - quite a collection - to my mind it will have a value for collectors, but it has gone to the boys - our grandchildren - however he set this one aside long ago. He showed me once. It's the match scorecard for the day when you and he went to the last day of the Test Match at Lords in 1975 - and it's got his pencil notes - 'disappointing day - went with G  he not impressed'."

"I remember it", said Sir George taking the envelope and putting it unopened into one of his jacket pockets. "I was honoured to be a such a famous place but I wasn't in tune with the day at all - the fanaticism of watching a sport which moved at a snail's pace passed me by. Harry never invited me again!"

"I was glad about that -because  the next year Harry  took me - I've kept that scorecard!"

"That would have been the week after I took you sailing - remember?"

"I'll never forget! I don't think I was ever so humiliated before or since - sorry."

"We had rather a row I think."

" I felt you were auditioning me for a marital role!"

"I never intended that! Am I forgiven?"

"At this distance - of course But it meant I chose  Harry. I'm a Yorkshire lass with cricket in my veins and  we were together ever after. I knew he was going places and that he was a rather sickly type - I was lucky to have him for so long."

"Odd how chance can influence one's life  I met Susan by chance at a regatta - like me she had small craft sailing in her family - only  in Norfolk in her case. In fact,  so much so that her parents named their children after characters in the in the Arthur Ransome books and she was Mate Susan! She seemed to like the fact that I could handle a small craft instead of just dressing up and pretending. I was delighted to find someone who knew what everything was for and how to use it –

"-unlike me then!"

"Water under the bridge Janet –our paths divided but I shall treasure the scorecard as a reminder of a remarkable man."

"Thank you George. Shall we just say that today is now and leave the past in the long- ago file."


Nodding in grateful assent, Sir George changed the subject. "I gather that Corporal Tyldesley  - 'Tyd' as she likes to be known – has been quite a regular visitor here."

"Almost part of the family."

" Yet  when Borthwick was speaking last night over dinner - nice meal - amazing what a country pub can do on a good night – he asked me how I'd found her – I said she seemed OK though given to speaking rather brusquely."

"Well she IS a bit Lancashire!"

"Borthwick said they were worried about her grasp of reality – she had apparently invented a girl friend called Ann in Blackburn."

"She has a fund of stories. I wonder if  the good Colonel
and those specialist experts he brought in really know her?
She's been coming here for ages now – I think Borthwick
was wanting to keep an eye on me and kept inventing
errands for Tyd – and Mrs W took her under her wing. I
gather Tyd poured out her heart to Mrs W."
" I can envisage that."
"Mrs W's  grandkids called her the 'funny lady'."
"Did they mean 'funny' as in "peculiar" or in "humorous"?
"Oh the latter – it seems that one rainy day when she came
here and they were about – she took them off Mrs W's
hands and told them stories – all manner of things – she
must have a fantastic imagination – they're convinced that
toothpaste comes from mines in Bexhill on Sea!"
"Bexhill? Where did she get that from?"
"It is where I'm moving to be with my sister  next month.
Tyd would have heard the name from Mrs W – I shall miss
them both but it is time for a clean  break.  Anyway, she
kept them quiet for ages – you know in 20 years' time she
might be one of our leading children's writers!"
"All rather beyond me, I'm afraid."
"Yes – I can see it is!"
Lady Janet's  manner became serious. She had something
to say she had bottling up for a long time.
"That day at Lord's you trashed something Harry held dear
– his cricket – he was too sickly ever to play but he threw
himself into the game emotionally – and you could not see
that – you were young of course – but you had done much
the same with me  - you did not see how unhappy I was in
that boat."
"I'm better with physical situations."
"Agreed George. Now - I have to say it – Harry believed
that you had a world class understanding of how the human

frame worked and how that could be replicated but  you have no idea of how people work. It showed right at the start  with me. You were dealing with a lass from a West Riding  mill-owning family knowing  nowt about boats– but we have learnt– the hard way - folk  are more than machines.”

“That seems self-evident but it’s the machinery of the human body which has been my lifetime’s work.”

“Wasn’t it just!  I watched you with your wife at the Reception for the Great and Good after the Memorial Service -”

“- It was excellent. You must have felt proud -”

“-I doubt if you’ve any idea how I felt but I watched your Mate Susan holding on to you and basking in the reflected glory of your fame – yes, I expect she’s had everything stowed in the right locker all your life – she’s been your what d’you call it? – First Lieutenant – hasn’t she. She’s given to you all these years – just you make sure, George – in the retirement years - she gets a bit back.”

“Rest assured I will make it my priority.”

“ Right. I’m sorry if you’ve found this a bit strong -I’m a northern lass – we speak as we find  - Coronation Street – Emmerdale - even that daft Last of the Summer Wine – there’s a grain of truth in all those. Harry could handle all that. Even though he became a baronet by the back door he was still a good man. He was proper pleased you got your knighthood – he reckoned you deserved it. So you and your Mate – sorry Lady -Susan - I wish you both fair winds and calm weather.”

“Well -er -thank you” was the reply from a now rather startled Sir George.

“And – one last thing  - you DO know about Tyd don’t you?”

"Borthwick rather skirted round her case. She was slightly wounded in Afghanistan but then had some sort of mental trauma  - not my field at all. The limp is apparently psycho -somatic."

"I think she felt she was at the Unit under false pretences as her problems have been mental rather than physical. But she can move on now. I like to think we here have been a help." She continued, reverting to her previous determined tone, "I think you should know about her".

In the minutes that followed, Sir George sat transfixed as his hostess explained the history of Corporal Tyldesley, adding more tales of her interaction with Mrs W's grandchildren including, of course, her displaying some remarkable prowess in garden cricket.

Then, with an air of finality, Lady Janet stood. "Shall we find your driver?" she suggested sweetly.

As though in a dream, Sir George followed his hostess through the house to find Tyd and Mrs W. He went through formal goodbyes and found himself sitting in the car again with a cheerful Tyd chattering on about Mrs W and her grandchildren.

Not since his paternal grandmother had upbraided him over some perceived lapse in behaviour as a teenager had he received such a dressing down. How he must have misjudged Janet all those years ago when she had turned out to be what Arthur Ransome, in the books he had devoured as a boy, called a "duffer"! And then Tyd's story had been a revelation.

He regained his composure. His driver was asking him something.

"Sorry Tyd", he said, for some reason addressing her directly by the nickname  for the first time. "I was miles away."

" I said – did you have a good afternoon?"

"Well – it was instructive – shall we say. Instructive but – most of all - helpful."

Helpful  - for he now had  tale to tell when it came to his "Retirement Speech", to remind all present that there are different sorts of rehabilitation. *There is more to life than even our brilliant prostheses,* he could say. He could tell a story of how he had met a young soldier, proven in battle but  forced into an unprecedented period of inactivity after being wounded thus entering a period of introspection  and self-discovery culminating in a decision which would bring personal challenges as great as any faced on the battlefield. Corporal John Tyldesley had transitioned into Jane Tyldesley. And a lot of the evident success of that transition had come about from the support, not of highly qualified clinicians but of  two women's common sense and understanding. There existed more than one sort of interdisciplinary team.

Helpful also– in that in that a light had dawned. He now saw goals for that retirement  which he had previously viewed with foreboding.  He had to  find a way to return to Susan  for her devotion. Also retirement might give him the chance to study how people's minds worked as well. There was so much he had yet to learn.

His mind still reeling, Sir George decided it would take time before he could tell whether or not it had been a GOOD AFTERNOON.

# AUTHOR'S POSTSCRIPT

Apologies for a swerve away from my more light-hearted themes but I wanted to pay my respects to the UK's Armed Service Personnel. I also wanted to remind readers of the amazing work of the Medical Profession in caring for the broken bodies and troubled minds of those who had risked their lives for others. The setting for this Tale has also given me a chance to draw attention to the enlightened approach of the UK Armed Services towards their serving members who experience Gender Dysphoria.

And in a lighter tone, for the record:

(1) Mines in Bexhill? No! Though exploration once found brown coal in the locality, the nearest example of the extractive industry is some few miles away where the product is not toothpaste but gypsum.

(2) For my friends at Lord's trying to recall the Second Test in that 1975 Ashes Series which was won 1-0 by Australia, the scores were: England 315 & 436/7 declared Australia 268 & 329/3. Of that last day when Harry took George – I suggest that watching a side batting for a draw in the fourth innings on a placid pitch may not be the most exciting spectacle.

A note of thanks.

I acknowledge also the help given me in putting this Tale together by members of the Hastings & Rother Rainbow Alliance Trans Group, a support and social group supported by, and part of, Hastings and Rother Rainbow Alliance http://www.hrra.org.uk

# MAY 1951

"Good afternoon, Sir George."

The burly, ruddy cheeked man was standing in the doorway of the cottage and, having pushed the door  open, was rapping on it  with his knuckles as he called out.

"Hello Tom." Sir George appeared in his dressing gown and wiping the shaving foam from his face, though it was early afternoon. "We had a last- minute change of plan." He turned to call to his wife: "It's Tom Trevaskis, darling." There was a faint "*Hello Tom*" from within.

"Yes" continued Tom. "I saw the smoke and thought it 'd be Mrs Trevelyan getting the cottage ready for you London folk but then I saw the Rover so knew t'would be yourselves. I wasn't expecting you at Chyangweal  till late tonight."

"We drove down last night," explained Sir George. "We thought we'd avoid the Bank Holiday traffic – it worked well. We  had a good run but we've been asleep all morning."

"Well, now you're back west of the Tamar and very welcome," smiled Tom.

Lady Margaret appeared, also in her dressing gown.

 "Aren't we awful," she apologised. "We've slept all morning - just got the fire going – and Mrs Trevelyan will be along in a bit with the usual groceries. I'm afraid we've rather rushed you all but the roads are SO busy this time of year with petrol rationing over and neither of us are used to driving far any longer so we thought we'd have an all- night adventure."

"Good for you," said Tom. "So 'twas your car I must have heard first thing. I listen out a lot at present – there's been trouble in the village - trouble with Old Colonel Willerton up at the Hall."

# AUTHOR INTERVENTION

That's how I would have liked to write a tale in the fashion of the great writers whose noted works I have on my heritage shelves. It would be about an adventure  when Cornwall was Cornish and we went on family holidays to St. Ives which had the gasworks where the Tate Gallery is nowadays and the little steam train puffed round the curve above Porthminster Beach and the sun shone and world was bright and wonderful. ***But*** FAST FORWARD SIXTY PLUS YEARS  - it wasn't like that at all. No Sir George – that I ever met – and I went by train not driving a Rover. There was no "Tom Trevaskis" just a rather miserable Scouser and no "Mrs. Trevelyan" – just a rather dozy girl from Slovakia or somewhere. A rather undistinguished hotel may well have once been the home of a branch of the estimable Willerton family but it was not an  old Colonel who had troubles but a thin lady with literary ambitions. So, following practice, we should now have a new title thus:

## APRIL 2019

... because the second Friday of that month found me, struggling with a heavy suitcase, alighting from the noon train from Paddington on to a rather windswept platform at St. Erth. I do not rank a greeting of the type which opens all our chapters but we will re-start this one with a yell in my direction from a scruffy youth:

"Are you the bloke for this literary thing?"
Surprised by the abrupt approach and incongruous accent, I replied: "I suppose so! I was expecting to go to Penzance

but I got a text saying get off at St. Erth and we'll pick you up."

"Er - right then. They've sent me in the hotel bus to get you. They said I had to look out for a tall Scotsman, so I expected a bloke in a kilt playing the bagpipes like."

"Presumably, the tartan scarf gave you a bit of a clue?"

"Oh yeah – right! I hadn't noticed actually It was the tall bit I spotted. Er – the bus is  parked by the entrance over there so I'll give you a hand with yer case like. It's probably quicker this way than going all the way to Penzance."

"Thanks very much," I said gratefully, letting him trundle and then pick up the case ready for the overbridge. "The kilt is in the case but the bagpipes wouldn't come   - they don't like the haggis here – and your accent speaks more of Toxteth than Truro."

"Wavertree actually but me mother was from over the water."

"America?""

"No – Birkenhead."

And thus began a Merseyside monologue on the unfairness of life in general and his mother in particular which continued without hesitation or repetition until we reached our destination. I merely mention all this to show that this set the scene for a day on which I had to expect the unexpected.

The  Hotel  turned out to be much as expected and I was giving kilt and sporran due care and attention and just about to make a cup of tea when the phone rang. It was the central European girl in Reception.

"There is lady wants to meet you - she in lobby", was the brusque message. Accordingly, expecting the organiser, I went down to get another surprise.

The last person I expected to meet was Stella from Putney though with hindsight I might have expected her to be at a gathering of literary hopefuls. I first met her in the days when I was living and working in London and on an assignment with a charity where she was a volunteer. I was lumbered with her as my PA for she was the epitome of the problem volunteer – the enthusiastically ineffective. I took her under my wing, so to speak, for which the CEO thanked me when I completed my time there, and Stella, who had never been employed after that, annoyingly had kept in touch. It seemed she always just about to publish a novel and sent me her poems regularly, giving me cause to regret that I, out of good manners, had complimented her on her verse one morning in those days when her role in life was to bring me coffee and a copy of the Financial Times.

 She had remained ”Stella From Putney” over the years, still living with her widowed mother in that London Borough. I hadn't recognised her name on my copy of the list of attendees and she hadn't mentioned she was due to attend when she had battered my ear on the telephone a few weeks earlier. Although we had spoken and exchanged emails and texts, I had not set eyes on her in years. However, she had not changed from the apt description given her once by my Yorkshire friend, Jim: *"Eh! That lass is nobbut skin and bone!"* I reluctantly have also had to agree with Jim's shrewd observation: *"Tha'll have problems there, lad. Yon lass has tekken a shine to thee!"* Now she was standing in the foyer and clearly delighted to see me.
"I was so pleased and so amazed to see you were on the speaker's list," she gushed.
"Yes – I'm opening the batting tonight Gawd knows why but they they've picked up on the work I've done on the

Family Memoir that's just out and the story of how I found Dad's old camp in the Aussie bush. They think that I can shine a new light on writing – apparently –'Your Family History As A Source of Inspiration' - fair's fair - they might have something there! Actually I think I'm here because they couldn't find anybody else to traipse all the way to Cornwall on a Friday night out-of-season and on expenses only. But what the hell – I've had one of the great British train journeys - I get dinner, booze, bed and breakfast then back in London tomorrow night. All I have do is talk – and that's no hardship. It's an ego trip – as the boys at the local rugby club took delight in telling me - but a great life this Literary Lark. But I expect you know that!"

"Not really," said Stella.

"You here for the whole weekend?"

"Yes, my sister was very keen I came here. I was going to come up tomorrow morning but when I saw you were speaking after Dinner tonight; I changed my plans."

"I didn't think I had that sort of star billing!"

"Well you haven't really - that's tomorrow – I hope to get some real inspiration but I wanted to talk to you so I caught an early train down this morning. Can we go and get a coffee in the lounge?"

"Lead on lassie, lead on!"

So, with some sense of foreboding, I found a spot in a corner in the deserted lounge and she duly appeared with machine-delivered coffee and accessories and sat down opposite.

I said: "This is like the old days, you  - fetching me a coffee!"

"I hope it is  - because you were the one who always sorted out problems."

"That's what you said when you rang me last month! We did talk a wee bit then – about an hour if I remember – gave me cramp and a sore ear!"

"I'm so sorry but I need to talk again. it's about Ma, of course,  it's not got any better!"
"Look, I'm a retired accountant who's taken to writing family history in his retirement. I'm good with debits and credits, not cares and worries!"
"But you have always been the only one who I could go to with my problems."
"So it would seem. You'd best proceed then."

And proceed she did, with me thinking: *Why have I got drawn into this?* Her diatribe reprised all the problems she had – almost literally  - bent my ear with a few weeks ago. Her Ma had lost mobility and needed care that Stella could not provide. Her sensible sister, Cilla who was married to "Bob the Builder" whom Stella thought vulgar – was arguing about what to do with Ma. Bob had offered to fit a stair lift – then offered to turn downstairs cloakroom into a wet room and move Ma into the front room. She refused all these offers and refused Adult Social Care saying: *My family will look after me.*

Having met Ma and being now quite irritated by this repetition, I was determined to remind Stella of the event. "You brought Ma to a rugby match at Rosslyn Park years ago. If I remember right, the game went on too long, it was too noisy, the clubhouse was draughty, it was the wrong sort of gin ..... yes I've not forgotten that. Neither have all my pals at the club!"
I was determined to be blunt for my leg was hurting and I had not come all the way across the south of England for this. I could see tears welling up in her eyes. She had not expected this but I continued.
"Look Stella, I'm sorry to come the heavy but .. it's time you grew up. You and  your sister MUST decide. It all boils

down to just how much walking your Ma can do. If she can't
– it has to be a Care Home. You can afford the best! If she
has some mobility then - adapt your home and get one of
the care firms to attend. OR get her into Sheltered
Accommodation. Either way, you can afford the best."
Stella went back into the moaning mode which had so
irritated me during the phone call.
"But what will I do?"
I had a sudden insight.
"I reckon it's out of your hands. I think that your sister is
fed up with your shillyshallying and has packed you off
down here so her and her fella can assess matters and move
progress.  I'll bet your when you get back to Putney you'll
find your sensible sister has made it very plain to your very
selfish Ma what's good for her. OK?"
Stella was looking at me as though I had hit her. I had more.
"AND if you want to get your poetry or stories published –
do it yourself – I can give you the website names. And you
stop feeling sorry for yourself and begin living for yourself.
You weren't put into this world to be somebody's drudge."
The tears had come and gone. I paused, very aware I had
just done something traumatic.
"That's it, Stella - you cannot carry on the way you are. And
now I have to carry on. I've got to rehearse my wonderful
words and get into my kilt. And how about you make this
the first day of the rest of your life?"
I saw a sudden - almost miraculous - change in the lady.
Suddenly there was a glint in her eye and a corresponding
tensioning of the jaw muscles.  "Thank you" she managed.
To my surprise, She suddenly rushed across, gave me a kiss
and a bony hug and then suddenly it was the agenda of the
weekend.
"What are you actually going to say tonight?"

"Well – I shall follow the Golden Rule: Tell 'em what you're going to tell 'em; tell 'em; then tell 'em what you've told them. Then I shall sit down to either rapturous applause or a puzzled silence."

"I shall lead for the first whatever happens."

"I'm wondering whether to put in a rude joke about the difference between Edinburgh and Glasgow."

"You'll have to gauge just how drunk they all are."

"Aye. Now I must go," I said rising to my feet, without realising that a significant event had just taken place. "I may not get to see you at the Reception, I'll be too busy with the Organisers – who at this moment are probably wondering why they've invited me."

Back in my room, faced with the cumbersome job of getting into the kilt and puzzling over how I would react to either of the receptions I had suggested & whether to include the rude joke, my mood was suddenly lifted. In speaking about my uncertainty over the inclusion of something rather risqué, for the first time in all our verbal transactions, Stella had actually made a suggestion! She had asserted herself with an opinion! Perhaps this really was going to be the first day of the rest of her life. My weekend might just have a useful outcome This wasn't just an ego trip anymore, I had done somebody some good! It had been a GOOD AFTERNOON.

## AUTHOR'S POSTSCRIPT ...

... is probably unnecessary here other than to remind the reader that this small book is a collection of fictional tales - each one with a basis of fact. As to the rude joke ...

# OCTOBER 2018

"Good afternoon, Sir George."

The greeting came as something of a surprise to Sir George as the smartly uniformed and clearly well-informed staff of the Train Operating Company helped him exit the First-Class carriage at the rear of the 1330 Glasgow -bound departure from London Euston which had made a timely arrival at his destination. "Welcome back to Preston" followed in the well-remembered regional accent.

Clambering aboard the mobility vehicle for the journey along the length of Platform 3 and up the exit ramp and through the entrance hall to where his daughter, Sarah, would be waiting, Sir George wondered just how many times he would have made the journey up this part of the UK's West Coast Main Line in his lifetime. He would have travelled thereby as a schoolboy, home for the holidays with his parents waiting to drive him to the big family house in the Fylde. He would have done similar as an Oxford undergraduate, changing here for the local train on the line to Fleetwood. Then later, on as a rising young academic in London, perhaps once more requiring a lift after the local station closed. Once, memorably, with his bride-to-be to show her the family home and a few years after, with a new daughter to show to the grandparents. Then, far too soon after that, two trips so close together, for the funerals of his parents.

His latest one, just a few years previously, was entirely different. The local university had discovered that the recently knighted London-based university professor whose team had just made a significant scientific breakthrough was actually a local lad  from just down the A585  and had invited him to give a celebrity lecture. But on all previous visits he had known what sort of reception he was coming to and now, as he was wheeled to a meeting with an estranged daughter, recently widowed,  he was far from sure.

His reception had occupied his mind for some time. The Carers who had ruled his life since his accident in May, had grudgingly accepted that he was now fit enough to accept the invitation to spend some time with Sarah at what he supposed must be a quite sizeable estate in the Ribble Valley, in Lancashire. It was an area he knew from childhood through family excursions to the western fringes of the Pennines from their large well-appointed home in the pleasant flat country that lies between Preston and the Irish Sea. But  the ongoing feud between mother and daughter whose origin -something to do with religion - still puzzled him, had precluded any previous such invitation. When one came at the New Year, he was delighted to accept but then came the accident and he was going nowhere!

During the trip, he had tried to busy himself with newspapers and a crossword but despite a drink of coffee, had nodded off - probably the result of a sleep deprived night and the painkilling pill which his Carer had insisted he take. He came to with a start to see that the train was rushing through Crewe Station.

The preoccupations of the previous night  made an unwelcome re-appearance. He had decided he was going to have to reprise the situation when he had to tell a successful PhD student that she was not going to get her Research

Fellowship. That was one of those occasions when he was forced to begin with the words: *"There's no easy way of saying this ..."*. Somewhere along the line, he thought, he would be saying that to Sarah.

Then what would happen if she made the conventional suggestion that he come and live with them in the county of his birth? How could he explain that he no longer felt it was his home? Would she understand that there being no longer a railway station or administrative area with the double- barrelled name of which he had become so fond meant that felt his roots had been destroyed and that, now, he was a Londoner through and through?

Aware he was becoming preoccupied and generating anxiety, he forced himself to concentrate on  the journey and to try to recollect features which, long ago, a train-mad schoolmaster had told him he must look out for north of Crewe. Somewhere, he would pass over what at one time was the world's longest railway viaduct and then the  first ever  split-level railway junction. After stopping at Warrington, where the steel silos of the soap works tower over the train, he would cross the world's first ever inter-city railway – Liverpool to Manchester. *What date was that again?* Those names resonated so!

> *Manchester* - from where his father, a Chemical Engineer, had moved the family to Fylde on being promoted to Senior Management in the industrial complex round Fleetwood.
> *Liverpool* - from where his recently deceased wife had originated.

Now he was back to thinking about Patricia and remembering the words of his Ma who had remained true to her Lancashire roots and was never afraid of plain speaking. After her first encounter with his bride-to-be, she had commented: *"She's got a waspish tongue your lass, but you'll do well with her as your wife. She'll always give you the push you need and you'll be taken care of for the rest of your life."*

More "Shove" than "push" he thought! But he had indeed been "taken care of"  and that had meant he could concentrate on his academic work and then the research team which became almost an obsession. But that life management, which had sheltered him from every domestic crisis and had ensured every material comfort, had been suddenly taken from him a year since, as pancreatic cancer robbed him of his spouse.

When that end came, he had discovered exactly how he had been looked after in the previous years. The dying Patricia had remained the supreme administrator to the end leaving him a file detailing all the household processes, a document whose contents totally amazed him. For instance, he discovered that his shirts were washed  and ironed by a local laundry firm run by a lady called Cathy and that all the cleaning of their flat was done by Mrs. Haynes, an energetic lady whose peccadilloes Patricia outlined in detail. He found that they had become a very well-off couple, especially as Patricia had been the beneficiary of a legacy which had enabled the paying off of the mortgage on  their spacious, well-appointed flat.

Nevertheless he had begun to rely on Delia, his PA, for guidance on personal matters including some instruction on how to prepare simple meals. This latter he had found perplexing and had started to eat out more and then to patronise the local take-away food establishments – rediscovering a childhood love of fish and chips.

Importantly, he had begun to enjoy long restaurant lunches – one of which had made a lasting impact.

He had hoped against hope that Sarah would have attended Patricia's funeral but it was not to be and it had been Delia – whom his wife had cruelly referred to as "Delilah" – who had offered comfort. But he was happy that this invitation had made amends  and now he was to be reunited with his daughter. Of course he would hardly recognise her, having over the years  seen but a single image of her in the snap she enclosed in the ground- breaking card the previous Christmas.

As Sir George dismounted from the mobility assistance vehicle at the station entrance, he became aware of a tall woman waving from the open door of a parked Rolls Royce.  She was accompanied by a well -built cheerful looking man with a chauffeur's cap tilted on the back of his head. He strode purposefully across to the truck saying: "Good afternoon, Sir George. I'm Sam - let me help you," and then taking the case and trundling it to the limousine.

Sir George, making full use of his arm crutch,  followed Sam the few  steps across to the waiting vehicle to where his daughter stood.
The two stood in an embarrassed second's silence.
"Father," she said, rather awkwardly.
"Hello, Sarah," said Sir George who had rehearsed this moment mentally. "You're looking well."
 They gave each other a perfunctory kiss on the cheek as etiquette demanded. Sarah, well aware that her father had suffered an accident in the Spring, had not comprehended her father's loss of mobility, was now concerned as to his ability to get in the car.

"Can you get in ok?"

"Not a problem," replied Sir George rather inaccurately as he heaved his sturdy frame and arm crutch through the limousine door. Then, making full use of his good right leg and his re-discovered upper-bodily strength, he levered himself onto the cushioned seat and shuffled  across to sit behind the driver's position, panting with the exertion all the while. Sarah followed him to sit alongside as Sam dutifully shut the door and moved round to take the driver's seat in the chauffeur compartment.

"How's the leg?"

"Still wobbly but the physio is doing wonders."

"I'm still not clear how you did it."

"Oh, I was being the absent- minded professor. Crossing the road. Walked in front of a delivery van. Poor fellow had no time to stop. He was terribly upset. His front bumper – what the Yanks call a fender – gave me one heck of a crack. Sheared off the top of the tibia. I'm all held together with metal."

As Sam eased the Rolls out into the Station Approach, there were a few seconds of silence with each wondering where the conversation would go next.

"I didn't know you had a Rolls!" began Sir George.

"Typical Tommy – had to show off," replied Sarah as the Rolls purred up the station approach and awaited its turn to turn right into Botchergate  "But it goes next month after the girls have gone back to school. I use a little Peugeot but we're getting a Range Rover – much more suitable for living in the country and just as comfortable."

Inevitably she moved to the  question posed since the dawn of civilisation to every traveller on arrival at their destination.

 "How was the journey? OK?"

"Fine. The Assistance worked splendidly. Very comfortable and quiet in First Class – though I don't think I would want to be a tall person in a Pendolino. Nice to be back on the West Coast Main Line – even though it's difficult to see through the windows. Lots of memories. Did a lot of thinking."

"I've been thinking too," replied Sarah.

"I always hoped you might do that – you were brought up that way!" smiled her father. "Your thoughts first then."

"Well," Sarah began cautiously. "By the way, that screen is entirely sound- proof so Sam can't hear a thing. I have to use the intercom to talk to him. Father ..."

"It used to be 'Dad'. Could you manage that?"

"Well, Dad,"  -Sarah used the word awkwardly – "we've both had big changes."

"Life changing," agreed Sir George, echoing the phrase used by his Carers and his friends and colleagues but whose full import he had been slow to realise.


"Exactly! So - there are things which must be said and I've always spoken my mind ... "

"You got that from your maternal Grandmother!"

"Like as not - but what has to be said should be said and no hanging about! I intend you to have a holiday so we'll say what has to be said right now."

"You *have* inherited that streak then  - I hope you haven't inherited that addiction to tobacco!"


"No way! Listen Dad, I've taken a number of decisions about my future. I intend to stay on at The Hall. Tommy left me very well off. I have the house and grounds, a lot of shares, capital from a huge life assurance pay-out -oh! - and a flat in London that I'm selling - in fact, I am a rich lady."

"That brings its own problems."

"Not as many as you might think. Tommy had a whole team of 'Wealth Managers' and 'Private Bankers' and it's all continuing."

"I am delighted to hear that – I had wondered how you were coping."


" I've run my own life for some years, Tommy was rarely at The Hall and I have lived the life of the Lady of the Manor – and I rather like it. When you see The Hall, you'll see why. The gardening is all looked after by contractors, Sam does odd- jobs and his Mum and his aunt clean and cook when I need them. Running all that occupies my time and we have the annual village fair and charity do on our lawns and organising that is a full-time job and very satisfying too. I know you  - with your life in London with your clubs and theatres and everything  - would find it all very dull, but it all suits me down to the ground."

Sir George looked at the confident woman alongside him, once the baby he had cradled in his arms, then the determined  little girl in pigtails, then the surly moody teenager and then the defiant rebellious young adult. He recognised none of them. Instead he saw a woman who bore some physical  resemblance to his late wife – though without the scowl and pursed lips - a stranger offering friendship. One who could call him 'Dad' but one whom he would have to get to know all over again. To his surprise, he found the prospect appealing.


Struggling again to find something to say, Sir George found a happy escape in a suddenly remembered promise.

"Sorry," he said, extracting a mobile phone from inside his jacket. "I promised to text my Carer to say I've arrived safely" and for the next few minutes he was busy struggling with the unfamiliar device. Then with a sigh of relief, he put the phone away once more and peered out of the car windows. They were travelling eastwards along the A59 and thus heading in the opposite direction from his childhood home.

"This town has changed a bit."

"It's a city now – er - Dad!"

"Of course – they took great pleasure in telling me that when I came up to the local University."

"I didn't know you were going to do that until I saw the local rag."

"They did me proud! I didn't know I was that good."

"Neither did your grand-daughters. They won't be home till next week and then it'll be a flying visit  - they're off somewhere again."

"I look forward to meeting them."

"And they you  --but I have to ask you not to discuss their father with them. Is that Ok?"

 "There were upset over his sudden death, then?"

"It would be nice to say 'yes' but untrue. They detested the man. They saw him as a noisy uncouth bully – and they weren't far wrong. But he had the Midas touch and the City financiers loved him. No – that's a bit far. The man created a climate of fear wherever he went, so he was respected if not liked."

"But you seem to have done well."

"I was his window dressing. And of course, starting as his nurse, I was one of the very few who had ever seen him vulnerable."

"So you got rich through Nursing after all!"

"Yes. Indirectly. Despite what Mother prophesied! Having said that – he gave me status and wealth I couldn't have earned myself – and of course, along the way, I came by two right little madams as daughters."

"Jayne and Marilyn!"

"Such common names – I know, But nothing common about them I assure you!"

Sarah drew a deep breath  and continued: "Dad, there's no easy way of saying this".

Sir George repressed a gasp – his daughter had pre-empted him!

Sir George had last seen that look in his daughter's eyes when, as a teenager, she had said: *Dad, I don't want to go to university. I want to be a nurse.* This time her words were just as convincing as she continued:  "Tommy was given to violent sadistic homosexual acts – but  he had whole team dedicated to keeping him out of the papers. They explained his absences by saying he was a migraine sufferer. Thing is- MOTHER KNEW! She was upset when I chose Nursing, though happy  when I went into the Private Sector. She was pleased that I married my richest patient but when I told her what I quickly found out about Tommy, she insisted that I left him immediately. I of course refused; I wasn't going to throw away that lifestyle just because of the peccadilloes of the moneybags I'd married . Looking back, I suppose I did that just to spite Mother and show that I could do well without going to University."

 Sir George recognised that a key point in his  life had just been reached. The future relations between him and this rather likeable daughter were going to depend on how he handled the next few seconds.  The numerous panegyrics which had accompanied the announcement of his knighthood mentioned scientific insight, clear sightedness, tactical expertise and so on. Tact and diplomacy were not mentioned. Aware of that, he began to pick his words very carefully.

"Why didn't I know? It might have saved a great deal of worry", he said, his mind racing with stratagems for the ensuing conversation.

"Mother said we must not tell you. You would not understand. You had to be shielded from the world to get on with your academic life. You were bound for greatness and she was going to get you there. She told you that tale about Tommy forcing me to join his church to cover up why she never spoke to me again."

"And, of course, – given her strict Nonconformist background - I believed her. But I grieved nonetheless."

Mightily relieved that he wasn't going to let a cat out of the bag after all and all that worry  had been unnecessary. Sir George felt it was his turn for candour,

"After you fled the nest to go into Nursing, Patricia made it clear ours was a business partnership and I accepted that. As you clearly owe a lot to Tommy, I owe a lot to Patricia. Without her I wouldn't have made it to the top – have led a research team in making a breakthrough – got a knighthood – she always said that she wouldn't rest till I got the reward I deserved – well I got it all and now she's at her rest."

To Sir George's surprise, Sarah leant across and squeezed his hand. "Dad, I knew everything about Tommy. Everything. Did for years. I know there was a young person with him when he died. I hate to say this but I'm almost glad he's gone. Now there's an end to it. A start to something new. OK? Only one thing – Marilyn and Jayne have not been told that Tommy was not their natural father. They'll learn that in the fullness of time so I'll thank you not to mention it."

The Rolls turned off main road and headed north.

"Nearly there now Dad – you'll soon be able to see The Hall."

Sir George felt that the time had come to end candour and the full story of how he had come by the accident was best left untold. The truth was that, after a long lunch with colleague whose fortunate choice of marriage partner allowed him a lavish lifestyle in a Chelsea Harbour block of luxury flats. Sir Geo suddenly realised that the person whose decadent doings had been the subject of his colleagues stories for some years and had been recently found dead in a comprising situation was actually his SON-IN-LAW!! The realisation came so hard to him that he was almost in a trance as he left the restaurant. The result was that, in attempting to cross the street, he walked out from behind a parked vehicle straight into the path of a white van proceeding on its lawful occasions  - fortunately in this case -at a very low speed but one still great enough to cause what the A&E Department called a "bumper fracture". That was all best left unsaid.

Suddenly, he felt relaxed. He was not going to be faced with telling an estranged daughter unpleasant facts about her late husband. She had not made any sign of wanting him to move into the Hall. His anxieties had proved groundless.

Sitting listening to his daughter reeling off the difficulties she was having with organising her annual event, he felt comfortable in the tide of trivia which was washing over him.  Then, seeing out of the car window the outline  of Longridge Fell where his father had once taken him to show him there was a world outside of his beloved Thornton Cleveleys and the Fylde and why he had leave it to go to school in the far-off English Midlands, he had one of those insights for which he was famed.

Now, at last, he could live for himself and not always to be doing something to please someone else. It started with his parents pushing him to achieve at school - by nature of his short-sightedness – that meant in academic terms and not on the cricket field in a game he became almost obsessed with. Then he had to succeed at Oxford to please them, then he had to marry, and then produce a grandchild. Then, of course, he had a wife who was determined to advance the career of her husband and schemed endlessly so that he would rise to hold a university Chair and then be awarded a knighthood.

He could get to know his daughter and perhaps even the two 'young madams' who were his grandchildren. He would give the Annual Memorial lecture in January when he would announce his retirement. Then he would have his summers, maybe coming back to Lancashire and the Ribble Valley but definitely spending time at Lord's enjoying the slowly unfolding pattern of county cricket in that most genteel of surroundings. In winter he could meet up with his university pals at weekends and enjoy rugby. And to do all of that, he would not have to leave the Bloomsbury flat, with the British Museum to his south and the British Library to the north, where he had all the creature comforts he needed and where he was so attuned to the way of life. And of course, there would be Delia.

And after all his worries – it was turning out to be a GOOD AFTERNOON.

# AUTHOR'S POSTSCRIPT

In a wholly fictional Tale, all locations except "The Hall" are real. I doff my cap to the good citizens of the twin townships of Thornton and Cleveleys , now in "Wyre", whose euphonious  double- barrelled identity existed as a hyphenated  administrative unit from 1927 to 1974 and remains to designate a UK Post Town. The station of the same name which our Sir George would have used, closed to passengers in 1970 but the eye-catching binomial can still be found in the lists of Rugby Union Football clubs.

I can personally assure readers that the "bumper fracture" which Sir George sustained in an absent- minded moment also is very real skeletal trauma to the upper tibia.

For the details of the West Coast Main Line, I am indebted to *Crewe to Wigan;* Adrian Hartless [Middleton Press2017] in particular, Note XII §50 which describes Dutton viaduct and Weaver Junction exactly as Sir George recalls. In seeking information about railways in the Fylde peninsula, to confirm he could have travelled as a student from a station called "Thornton- Cleveleys", I was well served by *Preston to Blackpool including Fleetwood;* John Matthews & Peter Fitton [Middleton Press 2018]

**Contributor's scribble:** *I am an engineer and cannot write stories so please read the following as a report from our first cruise of the season in our narrowboat.*

"Good Afternoon, Sir George."

My wife is not in the habit of addressing pub signs but, as we stood outside, we had both noticed the new sign fixed above the door of the canal side pub. It portrayed a very stern-looking 18th century gentleman.

[Please note that we do not make a habit of mooring alongside pubs but we had been forced to halt for a time having received notice of a blockage ahead of us.]

Moored ahead of us was the cabin cruiser that had preceded us out of the marina. It was crewed, rather inexpertly, by a young couple. *"Reckon they'll get as far as the first lock then remember what they came for!"* one of the marina staff had commented, winking at us, but they had not even made that. It was firmly moored with the hood up, the side-screens down and the saloon curtains closed. However it was exhibiting a regular rocking motion that could not have been the result of the wind. We both noted it but said nothing. *"If the boat's a-rocking' don't come a-knocking'"* was a tip the marina staff gave us when we began cruising.

We went into the pub. It was empty save for the obviously new landlord behind the bar. There was a framed print hanging on the wall which clearly had been the inspiration for the image on the pub sign. My wife opened the conversation which I record below.

WIFE: Who was Sir George?

LANDLORD: Sir George Cumming. Local landowner. Bad tempered, randy old sod, by all accounts. No local girl was safe! Dead against the  building of the canal – had men attack the surveyors – and  forced the canal builders to come round this way so - but for him this pub wouldn't be here.

ME: It was the "Navigation" when we came past last time. The marina lads said it was terrible and the landlord was rude. So boaters never went in.

LANDLORD: Exactly! We had to rename the pub as it had got such a rotten reputation despite being in the middle of nowhere. We decided not to call it by the full name – Sir George Cumming– as that's the sort of name Wetherspoons use and that's not the image we want. So welcome to the "Sir George". What can I get you?


We made it our rule right at the start of our canal boating trips not to spend lunch times in pubs –save for Sundays – so our order was half a bitter for me and a tonic with ice and slice for my wife. The conversation continued.

LANDLORD: Me and the wife have just taken over. In fact we only opened for the first time yesterday  -only had the one customer – local character – the Major. We were going to wait till Easter but it's very late this year. I expect you've stopped because of that tree down. Saw it this morning when I was out with the dog I rang CRT right away.

ME: It will be this wind. We thought twice about setting out this morning – we've been in your local marina.

WIFE: Chap coming the other way in a canoe told us so we checked with the CRT – they ARE very good.

ME: You don't realise until you're a boater how the wind can affect you.

WIFE: This is our first trip this year.

ME: Three years back we took a canal holiday and that decided how we wanted to spend our retirement.

WIFE: So we bought the boat. We specified the design– my husband is an Industrial Designer – and it was fun watching her being built. But we discovered it's not all sipping glasses of wine like on those programmes you see on the telly!

ME: Lot of hard slog especially at locks.

WIFE: And seriously unglamorous  chores, like filling the water tank and emptying the toilet.

ME: Lots of things to go wrong on a canal boat -even a new one like ours. And tricky  things like charging your batteries and handling bottled gas. Engine's not like a car's either.

WIFE: She's 52ft long - big enough for two large-ish people and  we can go anywhere on the network – including rivers. At least when there's no blockages or stoppages.

At that point, the Landlord's wife appeared and joined in.

LANDLORD'S WIFE: You are our first boaters. Welcome. The previous chap hated boaters. The Cut's all rich men's toys he told us. You don't see working men on here but it was working men who slaved to build these canals now their descendants can't afford to use them.

LANDLORD: He used to say: all arty-crafty rich types on narrowboats and jumped-up posers on plastic pretend yachts. And he told his customers to their faces!

WIFE: After a hard day's boating – the toilet's playing up or the lock paddles are stuck ...

ME: .. or you've dropped your windlass in the Cut.

WIFE: Yes – well there's no need to remind me – but if you've had a bad day– the last thing you want is go into a pub and be insulted!

A bristling sort of chap came in who we knew to be the Major because the Landlord greeted him as such.

MAJOR: What ho, Landlord! Can't tell you how pleased I am to see this place open again. Half of the usual please.

They've cleared that tree branch. You two off that narrowboat outside?
US: We are!
MAJOR: Thought so. You look like narrowboat chappies. You'll be on your way then.

On our way it was indeed  but we were delighted to have actually gone into a country pub and met a "Major"! Underway once more, we chugged past the pub.
NOW ... it may have been a trick of the light but – as we passed - both my wife and I will swear that the picture of Sir George on the pub sign looking down on the rocking cruiser, winked at us. Perhaps the old rascal had spotted that at least two people were having a  GOOD AFTERNOON.

# AUTHOR'S POSTSCRIPT

Whilst commercial carrying continues on navigable rivers and Ship Canals in the UK, the country's Inland Waterways have reinvented themselves as a major leisure facility. At the time of our Tale the number of licensed boats on canals and rivers managed by the Canal & River Trust **(CRT),** who succeeded the state-owned British Waterways in 2012, was over 34,000.  Many of them would be leisure craft, in the style of the commercial **narrowboat** that was the traditional working boat of the English canal system where the width of the locks determined that a craft be no more than 7 feet wide.
 N.B. They should NOT be referred to as a "barge".
**Paddles** are valves of various types that regulate flow of water into and out of canal lock chambers.
A **windlass** or "lock key" is a detachable crank used for opening lock paddles. A vital tool for a boater so it is not a good idea to drop yours into the canal or "the Cut" as it is sometimes nicknamed.

Whereas the author hath previously and by sundry literary means sought to entertain with tales relating to matters experienced within his own lifetime, he hereby gives notice that the following pages may detain the attention for a longer period and will transport the reader's imagination to

# OCTOBER 1829

# OCTOBER 1829

"Good afternoon, Sir George."

The greeting, chorused by the three occupants of the room in The Lion Hotel, was not one redolent of enthusiasm. Indeed, expecting such a welcome, Sir George had paused outside in a moment of reflection before he tapped on the door with his silver-topped cane. He was aware, from the letter he had received requesting his presence, that something was amiss and that matters had somehow not lived up to expectations. Furthermore, he was arriving well after the time appointed for the meeting. Taking a deep breath, he had pushed open the heavy door and became immediately aware that being attired, as he believed, befitted a well-off country squire, he was in sharp contrast to the workaday drab of the townsmen. He was immediately reminded of the similar situation in the August of the previous year when to his great surprise the local Rector had written to him in a beseeching tone asking him to preside over a meeting of townsfolk who wished to promote a new railway.

From that time, he recognised all the three faces but could only put a name to one, the banker Mr. England with whom he had previously transacted business and it was he who rose in welcome.

"Sir George, we are honoured once more that you grace our presence in this humble town. May I present Mr. Higginson, proprietor of more than one of our local manufactories and our man of learning, Mr. Roy. Let me take your hat and topcoat and pray, sir, join our table.”

Duly divested of hat and overcoat, Sir George seated himself on the bench by the table which bore ample evidence that his companions had already taken full advantage of the provisions he was pleased to see had been laid out on a sideboard. Laying his cane across the table on top of his carefully folded gloves and very conscious that an apology was due, he began:
“Gentlemen, I am aware it is well past noonday and I must straightway apologise for my tardiness. We were much delayed by farm carts on the turnpike and then by my lack of knowledge of your town. My coachman took me to the inn wherein we held that meeting last year and we have had some trouble finding this excellent venue. The local urchins seemed to find great delight in pelting my carriage with mud! Fortunately, I see the victuals I ordered from the local provision merchant have indeed found the right target!”

“And most welcome they are,” commented Roy who had moved to the sideboard and was slicing portions of cold roast mutton and cheese to serve their visitor. “You will take a tankard of our local ale; I trust Sir George. We thank ye for your largesse in this provision of tasty delicacies.”
“I note the cheese has the Cheshire stamp,” said England.
“From my own estate,” explained Sir George.
“Indeed,” replied the banker. “And more welcome in this town than the product from Leigh.”
“The Leigh cheese does toast well,” countered Higginson. “I had occasion to sample their wares on a recent visit to admire their new railway.”

"Railways, indeed. The preoccupation of the age!" said Sir George who had begun to tackle the food with some gusto as the hour of day had sharpened his appetite. "I see, Mr. Roy, you have a copy of this enactment which I thought had settled the matter but, I am given to understand, is not to the satisfaction of the town and is the reason I am recalled to your presence. And that presence – if I understand the affair correctly – is somewhat lacking in persons."

"It is our turn to express regret, Sir George," said England. "There indeed should be two more persons to our company but we are given to understand that Mr. Dickenson, our land agent and surveyor, and Mr. Riley, our general merchant – a man most assiduous in the promotion of his wares - are to join us presently."

"I did but yester evening send my man, Simcock, to the dwellings of both gentlemen with a reminder that we convene here and not at the earlier venue of the Nag's Head inn. They are energetic young men- doubtless out and about on horseback - but are to be trusted," Roy added.

"In any case, to my understanding, we are met but informally," smiled Sir George.

"Indeed we are,  Sir George, and thus I am not provided with quill and ink," said Roy. "But our deliberations have import. Let me remind all as to our intentions when setting out on this enterprise. If you will indulge me, Sir George, I quote from the wording of the legislation in whose enactment  you played a noble part."

Balancing his spectacles on the end of his nose and taking the sheaves of printed matter in his hand, Roy began: "I paraphrase the wording, but when we, in this town,  set out on this enterprise we believed our railway to be: *"a work of great public utility and advantage by opening a safe convenient and expeditious communication for the conveyance of goods wares and other merchandise between the said town and the towns of Liverpool and Manchester and other populous places and also affording a cheap and quick conveyance of coal from the pits in the neighbourhood."*

He looked in the direction of Higginson and continued: "The very apposite note regarding coal is made - that in our town.. " *large quantities are consumed both for domestic and commercial purposes .."*
"Quick conveyance of coal," cried Higginson. "For myself, that is  the principle which enjoins us to provide our township with this most commodious form of travel: the railway with steam powered locomotives. The acclaimed outcome of the late competition at Rainhill surely proves my point!"

"Although laboured in the usual way of lawyers – the words express a  worthy aim indeed," acclaimed Sir George. "As ye all know, I am not of this town, though by the courteous instruction of Mr. England here, I now have local financial interests. To me, and to my brother in my native north east – I consult him in all these matters - it makes great sense to make this short connection to  the new railway which Geordie Stephenson is presently constructing between those two growing centres of commerce. Be assured gentlemen, I am convinced that iron wheels on iron rails are the future and not cartwheels on rutted roads."

"We are all in accord in that aim in the generality of things," said England. "But there are matters here, in particular which concern me. Sir George if you will indulge me whilst I air those concerns."

"Pray do, sir," smiled Sir George. "You are our man of Finance; I am but a simple country squire."

"I am indebted, Sir George".

Sitting back in his chair, and clasping his hands in front of him, England duly expounded: "I believe that after the wheel and the steam engine, the joint stock limited liability company is the greatest invention of mankind. It is certainly the way in which we will fund these new transport enterprises. However, I remain unconvinced that funding by the selling of shares will be sufficient even if this new railway company succeeds in calling all the capital. Borrowing will be necessary."

Roy interrupted the flow: "And who indeed shall profit from that borrowing but the banks! I wish to hear no more of this at present and am minded, Sir George, that your coachman will be as in need of victuals as were we. I shall take some of this excellent repast to my man Simcock who is within these walls someplace and ask him - if he can draw himself away from the admiration of the Irish serving wench - to pass this on to your man. I shall beg writing materials from Mr. Peaker, our excellent landlord and return. Sir George, gentlemen, pray excuse me!"

When the door had closed behind him, Sir George felt inclined to comment; "I feel you may have hurt the feelings of our learned companion, Mr. England!"

"Take no heed of it," was Higginson's rejoinder. "Our man of learning lives in a land of books – the workings of finance and industry are foreign to his nature."

"But a generous nature, none the less," commented Sir George. "However, he may find that Harris, my coachman, has a practised way of providing for himself. That is the more so whenever there are comely serving lasses in the offing!"

England, in the meantime, had turned his attention to the printed sheaves which Roy had left behind.

"Ah here it is," he cried with a note of triumph. "My concerns have been recognised in the Act. Here we have, in Section Fifty-One, the sum which I recall one of our engineer guests – though my memory does not divine whether it were Mr Stephenson or Mr. Locke – informed us as to be the cost. It is – as you may well remember – a total of forty-three thousand, four hundred and seventy-eight pounds. A remarkably precise sum to my mind."

"I feel that the sum may be the outcome of Mr. Locke's determinations," said Higginson. "He strikes me as the more precise of the two."

"And as a Yorkshireman, not easily dissuaded from his opinions," remarked England, who was continuing to leaf his way through the papers. "But this Act before us provides that we raise the sum of fifty- three thousand pounds – a sum well in advance of esteemed engineer's estimate."

"Well then sir" cried Sir George. "I am not well versed in the ways of railroads and tramways, have not your capability with finance nor yet adept at Logic and Arithmetick but it seems that all is well with this enterprise. Pray what is the alarm that hath caused my drive to meet with you?"

 England resumed his locked finger pose and peered at Sir George.

"The matter is not as simple as it may seem, Sir George," he began. "There has been the unseemliest squabble over the allocation of shares in our new  Railway Company with much  spurious argument as to entitlement. This does not bode well for the financing of the project."
"Thus proving what we in the oft derided world of trade and industry so often say," interjected Higginson. "Coin is king."
"And it would appear the coin is lacking," said Sir George for whom matters had taken a worrying turn. *Had these gentlemen invited him in order to beg off him?*

England, sensing Sir George's mood, was quick to return to the pages of legislation and continued:
"That eventuality is provided for, Sir George. I see here – it is in Section Sixty- Two and it does authorise borrowing to the extent of some twenty thousand pounds against the security of the property of the Railway."
"Then all is well surely in that respect" replied Sir George, somewhat relieved. "I do not yet see the purpose of my being here."

"Your entire purpose in this venture is indeed obscure to me," said Higginson purposefully. "I dared not ask earlier for fear of appearing ignorant before our learned and temporarily absent friend but why are ye come amongst in the first place? I know you presided over the meeting in the Nag's Head and did so with great presence of character and to great effect for I saw ye speak with the railway engineers. I understand also that it was with your furtherance that this great dollop of apparently necessary law was spawned. But ye are not of our town, did not attend at the unfortunate First General Meeting on Fourth of June last and just now abjured any claim to particular knowledge – so: what is your purpose being amongst us?"

Sir George had prepared himself for being questioned so directly and was prepared.

"My purpose, as you describe it, came about as a total surprise. Your Rector wrote to me in a most beseeching tone last year asking me to preside over a meeting of townsfolk apparently to reconcile two opposing factions and bring about the construction of a new tramroad or railway. He seemed to be of the belief that I, being originally from the north east, had special knowledge in such matters and was acquaint with Stephenson and such like persons. I assented, of course, - to the point of promising my earnest endeavours - but stated you would be better served by my younger brother. How he knew about me, with my dwelling halfway across the next county remains a mystery to me."

"Ah," said England. "Let it be a mystery no longer for 'twas I who put him up to it. I recalled our meeting - back in'25 was it, Sir George? – when you had lately come into your inheritance and spoke of your north-east connections. When our rector came to me in July last year after two separate meetings proposing a railway were held at one time and asked how we might bring these two rivals together, it occurred to me that you would be our man."

Sir George was somewhat alarmed and his reply echoed his thoughts:

"I hope and pray, Gentleman, that you have not overestimated my power and influence in such matters."

"Indeed," said Higginson, firmly. "I hope not. However, I remain in the dark as to the origins of your connection with our town."

"I trust Mr England; you will allow me to recall the genesis of our acquaintanceship .." England, now in a rather bad-tempered mood, made a swift gesture of acceptance and Sir George continued. "I avow that I breach no confidence when I say that having come into  my title and lands in Cheshire some few years past and following the advice of my brother in my native north east of England, I decided upon investment in manufacturing."

"A wise move" interjected Higginson. "It is the future of our great and glorious realm!"

Sir George continued: "I quickly elucidated that participation in the local salt enterprises and the associated river trade were jealously guarded by the locals and had no place for a newcomer. I learnt also that I stood little to no chance of elbowing into established interests in the towns of Liverpool or Manchester. Hence I sought opportunities in the fast expanding town that lay between them. Accordingly I met with Mr. England here, a  banker highly recommended to me and in a most cordial meeting discussed many matters the outcome of which was indeed a fruitful investment. I do not believe that, at any time, I presented myself as an expert in the matter of the iron way."

"Nor did you, Sir George," agreed England. "However, I readily perceived that you had one precious property as far as we were concerned  - you were an out comer and a man in no way related to our local landowning families who are all intertwined by marriage or kinship. Thus I gave your details to our Rector believing you would be accepted as an arbiter of the most impartial sort."

"In that role, I own, you performed well," avowed Higginson. "And all have noted that you have no ties to local families, especially those who have combined to frustrate our purpose."
"Mr Higginson, it is my turn to be in the dark," stated Sir George.

England, sensing that matters were in danger of becoming heated, speedily interjected. "Being not of these parts, Sir George, you are clearly not aware that the Noble Lord and the Reverend Gentleman, who seem set against our enterprise, are related by marriage. The mother of our Baron Lilford, who, like yourself Sir George, has but recently come into his inheritance, is sister to the Reverend Hornby's wife."
"And both those gentlemen are the proprietors of most of the land over which our railway is planned to pass," explained Higginson further.
"So wherein lies the impediment?" queried Sir George, still rather puzzled concerning the whole matter.

"You did not attend the General Meeting which was duly called on the first Thursday in June," pointed out England. "I saw no point in my attendance," replied Sir George, firmly. "I do not propose to be a subscriber to this enterprise although I was happy to be an instigator. I came as requested to that meeting a year last August and at the close, all seemed well. I left matters in the hands of the engineers that they might proceed in their accustomed manner and asked that, out of manners, they inform my brother of progress."

"Then you have, in fact, taken no further interest!" Higginson exclaimed.

Sir George was peeved at this. "I took an interest, I heard that Parliamentary sanction had been obtained in May of this year. I also heard that Geordie had ordered the iron rails. But I did not feel I had any further connection and my energies have been diverted elsewhere."

"This despite our being asked by the meeting to be part of a small group who would supervise progress!"

Now it was England's turn to be surprised.

"I do not recollect that," countered Sir George.

"You do not remember Mr. Gandy the clog maker suggesting that two parties from each faction with yourself presiding and the ever- reluctant Mr. Roy as clerk, act together in the furtherance of purpose?" England's voice had risen in pitch.

"I recollect a funny little tradesman speaking in a quaint fashion but it had no import to me."

Higginson had almost reached a  growl: "Funny little tradesman and quaint in his speech he may be but he has one of the shrewdest minds in town. And we are here at his suggestion."

Sir George's surprise was evident. "How can that be!" he cried. " It was the Rector who wrote me, albeit in the vaguest fashion, suggesting all was not well and it was once more my duty as a Christian gentleman to meet with you. He defined a time and place and informed me of all who were desirous of my presence."

"Ah," said England. "I divine the hand of Mr. Gandy in this. We shared a pipe of tobacco sometime after that calamitous meeting and I know he was bent on seeking the Rector's assistance."

Sir George was becoming more and more puzzled. "Pray tell me, gentlemen, what is this calamity of which you speak?"

It was Higginson's turn. "Neither England nor myself attended on the inglorious Fourth of June but we are now – by word of mouth – both well acquainted with the transactions."

"Indeed," agreed the banker. "It appears that an agent of the contractors tried to conduct business but there was immediate disagreement over whether there were supposed to be fifteen or thirteen directors."

"I cannot see that the difference between those two numbers being of vital import," said the still puzzled Sir George.

"It matters greatly in this town," said Higginson, "but that was not the cause of discord."

"No indeed," agreed England. "It appears that, ere matters due for discussion could be put to the gathering, there was an interjection."

Higginson continued: "A young man of this town but with connections in the Mackerfield district took the stage waving papers such as we have before us."

"He goes by the name of Critchley," explained England. "I understand he is a man well-versed in modern science and learning. He asked all present if they were aware that the legislation of May prohibited the use of steam locomotives on the line."

"I think we may all judge the uproar," said Higginson. "Our new link by rail is to be nothing more than a horse driven tramroad! Can you imagine! The turnpike trusts will dance a jig and we should be the laughingstock of the folk from Wigan who are undertaking a similar connection without any apparent let or hindrance."

"Ah!" Light was dawning for Sir George. "Those personages of importance to whom you referred earlier have put a spoke in the wheels of progress."

Higginson had the sheaves of legislation in his left hand and he jabbed at it with his right forefinger.

"Here 'tis," he cried. "Exactly as young Critchley demonstrated. It is Section 17 which places a restriction on the use of steam engines across the lands of Lord Lilford and the adjoining parish of Winwick. As that comprises the greater part of our route our purpose is rendered futile. Indeed this whole sheaf of law is as much use as a water mill in the sands of Araby!"

"Then all is come to naught," moaned Sir George. "I feel I have neglected my duties here in favour of my own personal purposes."

"I too, I fear," said England. "I considered all to be well and attended to my profession."

"And I am also complicit," added Higginson. "Consumed with the problem of accessing coal supplies, I believed all to be well, placed in the hands of others. Especially one so distinguished by his finery and his grand carriage!"

"What said the meeting?" asked Sir George, who recognised the barb but decided to deflect matters.

"It was Mr. Gandy who settled matters, I understand," said England. "He called for the meeting to be adjourned and then called for we who were originally nominated to effect some sort of progress. But I fear – as evinced by the lack of attendance – that what we have deemed as progress is likely to be adjourned *sine die.* Perhaps this grand scheme of railroads which link towns rather than provide local links to our waterways is but a pipe dream. I cannot see that this enterprise can progress."

Sir George faced the other two in turn and addressed them with a determination in his speech.
"The collapse of your enterprise is of my doing. I readily excused myself from attention to the detail of the parliamentary business in favour of matters of the heart. I have prospered from my investments in your town but when you turned to me, in my ignorance, I let you down. I feel it is my duty as a Christian gentleman to defray those costs which the Stephenson's will surely place before you, note of which you may despatch and good time, though indeed that will surely wreak havoc with my marriage plans."
"A noble gesture, indeed, Sir George," said England. "But I feel it will not be needed as funds do exist and some reimbursement could be made if all is to be abandoned."

A gloomy silence descended on the three. Then Sir George, slowly rose to make his departure but had scarce gained his feet when, suddenly, the corridor without the room was filled with the sound of cheerful voices and the door was flung open.
In the doorway appeared Roy clutching, a quill and an inkstand in one hand, whilst holding a mug of ale in the other and struggling to maintain his grip on some sheaves of writing paper tucked in his armpit.

"Our young bloods are returned!" he cried. "And we have good tidings. Sir George, gentlemen, pray welcome Mr. Dickinson and Mr. Riley."

Two young mud- spattered men, carrying mugs of ale, pushed past Roy into the room and headed directly for the now rather depleted sideboard.
"Forgive our tardiness," gasped Riley. "We have just returned from a visit with our new friend the Rector and made a diversion to one of his Lordship's tenants."
Dickenson, alongside his young companion at the sideboard, looked over his shoulder to the others with an explanation: "We were not offered aught to sup  nor a bite to eat at either place. Nor aught for our  mounts. Ah indeed - forgive us- we bid you welcome Sir George."

"Your mounts will be soundly attended to," said Roy seating himself and arranging his materials. "Gus the stable boy is a rare man for horses. All will be well fettled there. Sir George, pray be seated once more for our work is about to begin."
"Then in the words of the noble Duke, it has been a near run thing, for I was about to send for my carriage and depart one and for all," asserted Sir George.
"A fine carriage it is too, "said Dickenson, having cleared the table and seating himself. "But your coachman and Mr. Roy's man, Simcock, appear to be contending for the favours of the same lady."
Sir George laughed. "When I inherited lands and title, I was schooled never to intervene in the private lives of servants," he averred.

Said England: "The redoubtable Mr. Peaker has his own peculiar way of arbitrating  and is well able to settle such matters – we need not worry ourselves on that account. The matter in hand, Mr. Riley, Mr. Dickenson, is that you clearly have tidings for us!"

The two late arrivals, having cleared the sideboard of its remaining provisions, took their places at the table and, with energy, began to tuck in to both their plates and their discourse. Riley was first to speak. "We shall eat and speak by turn. Mr. Roy, you are provided with writing material I see. That is for the good for I can announce progress and I foresee your glum faces will soon be aglow."

Dickenson took over. "We were both resolved to further matters after the shambles and shouting of the meeting in June and so took Mr. Gandy's expressed wishes to be our purpose which our trip this mucky morn should have fulfilled."

It was Riley's turn: "When we learned that the noble lord and the Reverend Gentleman had conspired with Parliament to pass an Act which in effect forbids the use of steam locomotives. we resolved to act on our own account." Then Dickenson continued: "We duly paid a visit to the Rectory and spoke to the Reverend Hornby and his good lady. She is named from a biblical queen and is indeed a person of surprising presence. She claims she spoke also for her sister's son, the noble lord himself."
"And we had little problem in believing that claim," added Riley.
Dickenson took over: "Mr. Riley is well known in the town for  having a persuasive way of speech and it was he, gentlemen, to whom we are indebted for inducing the

Rector to accompany us on a trip to the grand Railway Locomotive Trials at Rainhill earlier this month."

Riley took up the tale, with glee. "Our Reverend Gentleman amazed us all by showing total delight at the performance of steam locomotives. It was difficult to get him away from them! He claimed he saw the hand of God in their construction – 'Engines of the Lord' – he called them!"
"More to the point," continued Dickenson. "He promptly reversed his opposition to their use on our railway. Indeed, he was most insistent that we have plenty of them! His worry – though 'tis my opinion  it was that of his wife -was that the land would be clouded in smoke. You will presumably know, gentlemen, that the fuel for these locomotive engines has been through the coking process as used in iron smelting and gives negligible smoke."

Roy had resumed ownership of the sheaf of legal papers. "Aha!" he cried. "At a stroke we render Section Five of this unlovely enactment  - ludicrously it calls for engines to consume their own smoke – entirely spurious! Capital!"
"Such detail was  unknown to me," said England. "But apart from your giving the Reverend Gentleman a jolly day out pray tell us, what was the outcome of 't?"

"The outcome is this," said Riley, producing a document for within his jacket. "The Man of God has duly fulfilled the promise he made to us at Rainhill. With great expedition he has prepared a sworn statement. Mr. Roy, I give it into your safekeeping. Do please, read out the pertinent passage."
Roy, with evident satisfaction, took the document, adjusted his glasses and after a quick perusal, addressed the group.

"Gentlemen, attend to this paragraph: '*Whereas from recent Experiments it hath been proved to our satisfaction that the Use of Locomotive Steam Engines properly constructed may be permitted and that the same may pass through our aforementioned townships without being a Nuisance or Annoyance from the Noise of Smoke thereof or any other cause; we the undersigned hereby consent to the Repeal of so much of the Act of 17th May 1829 as prohibits the passage of Locomotive Steam Engines through the aforementioned townships.'* It bears the signature of the Noble Lord and the Reverend Gentleman."

"Then," said England, "I think we may claim a victory and indeed acclaim our two worthy young townsmen for their ingenious experiment."

There was a chorus of "Hear, hear!"

"It was a near run thing indeed," said Dickenson. "The ink was scarce dry on the paper and we had one further visit this morn which was the reason behind our tardiness."

"Indeed," explained Riley. "One of his Lordship's tenants had also put his oar in, claiming the railroad would block his path to the turnpike in time of flood. We met with him and he is a stubborn fellow indeed – although others may well have suggested he might have objections to the construction of the railway."

"Let us not become  bothered with that matter," said Dickenson. "Matters of wayleave can be attended to later."

"Indeed so," said Sir George. "But I trust that you  young men made it clear to the Reverend Gentleman that we are indebted to him and his kin for this welcome change of heart."

"That we did," said Riley. "I assured the Reverend Gentleman that the name 'Hornby' would long be respected amongst all who value railways."

"And I am indeed surprised that a man of the cloth should become so enamoured of the steam locomotive," said England.

"Gentlemen," said Higginson very firmly. "Despite these good tidings, we cannot yet claim a victory as the legislation still blocks our purpose."

Sir George was suddenly animated: "There is a path for us and on this occasion I pledge I will not leave matters unattended. Mr. Roy, charge your quill and I trust that Peaker's excellent ale has not dulled your wits. Take note for 'tis my belief, gentlemen, that all is needed is another Act but one which suits our purpose fully."

"A capital plan," cried England. "Lead us down this path, Sir George."

Sir George, delighted to be of use, warmed to his task.

"Note ye well then Mr Roy, the following," and he began to count points on his fingers. "First, the Act will repeal the prohibition of Steam Locomotives recognising the sworn Statement we have to hand. Second – for Mr. England the Railway Company is authorised to borrow moneys whether or not all the shares are subscribed, Up to a sum of how much, Mr. England?"

"Twenty Thousand Pounds would seem sufficient."

"Note that please. Mr. Roy. And now Mr. Higginson a northern branch to coalfields?"

"Indeed. We could well bridge the Liverpool to Manchester line and link with this proposed branch to Wigan. That would give access to the coal pits around Haydock and Orrell."

"Hold an instant, if you please Mr. Roy," interjected England. "It may not be wise to specify those locations. I do not doubt that something of note may one day come from Orrell but this is not the time to dignify the area with inclusion in public legislation. I take it all of you agree."

There was a muttered assent and Sir George continued: "In the matter of the disputatious farmer, Mr. Dickenson you have a suggestion?"
"A simple remedy occurs to me," was the reply. "If Mr. Roy would note that the tenant, - his name is Cawley - and his lawful heirs and successors to the tenancy be granted the right in perpetuity to access the lands of the Railway Company without penalty in time of flood."

"Excellent! We make progress," approved Sir George, who had remembered  a point of his own. "I recollect also that I promised Locke that when this line makes its junction with their existing track, he will have charge of it, for it is clearly a novelty and so the new Act will need to recite that also. So there, I believe we have it. Mr. Roy when your ink is dry I shall take your papers and take my leave of you but this time I promise that I, with the aid of my brother, will duly further the legislation. Be assured of it - but be further assured that these matters are not swift and ye should look to next Spring ere we have an Act to your satisfaction."

Hatted and coated and pausing before he took his leave of the group, Sir George had a last word for them.

"Gentlemen, this may well be the last  you see of me and the last that railway construction sees of me  and indeed possibly the last your faction-ridden, disputatious township sees of me.  As vouchsafed to you, I have followed Miss

Austen's principle regarding a single man in possession of a fortune and am to be married next Spring - by which time, your railway enterprise should similarly have reached a happy state. I bid you farewell."

* * * * * *

Mounting his carriage to trundle back over the turnpike south to  his Cheshire estate – and noting but not commenting on the discolouration around one of Harris's eyes – Sir George felt some mild elation. He had finally fulfilled his promise to the Rector and was about to rectify his sin of omission He could now proceed with a future as a married gentleman of substance and leave railroads and their locomotives safe in the hands of others. So, seating himself in the carriage he reflected that that it had been, for him at least, a GOOD AFTERNOON.

# AUTHOR'S POSTSCRIPT

The astute reader will have quickly gathered that the unnamed town of this tale is indeed Warrington, at that time a township in the County Palatine of Lancaster and nowadays a Unitary Authority within the ceremonial county of Cheshire. The "Newton in Mackerfield" below has since morphed into a more euphonious "Newton Le Willows".

The diligent researcher will find a way through the list of 19th Century Acts of the UK Parliament to where, under 10 Geo 4. cap37, we find:

*"An Act for making and maintaining a Railway or Tramroad from the Liverpool and Manchester Railway at or near Wargrave Lane in Newton in Mackerfield, to Warrington, in the County Palatine of Lancaster, and Two collateral Branches to communicate therewith." [14th May 1829.]*

which is that piece of legislation so derided by one of our group.

However, the listing also gives us a sequel under 11 Geo 4 cap. 57:

*"An Act to enable the Company of Proprietors of the Warrington and Newton Railway to extend the Line of the said Railway ; and for repealing, explaining, altering, amending, and enlarging some of the Powers and Provisions of the Act relating thereto.*
*[29th May 1830.] Powers of 10 G. 4. c. xxxvii. extended to this Act, except as hereby altered, §1. Repeal of the restrictive Clauses in 10 G. 4. c. xxxvii prohibiting the Use Locomotive Engines through Burtonwood and  Winwick."*

Thus our tale did have a happy outcome and – despite the time-consuming squabbling our Sir George foresaw – the  Warrington & Newton Railway ran a train to convey passengers to the Haydock Races in June 1831, being formally opened throughout in the following month.

## .. AND APOLOGIES AND EXPLANATION

In attempting to garland a trellis of fact with the blossom of fiction, I needed some characters to represent the successful men of Warrington who are my protagonists. Instead of sticking a pin in the telephone directory, I raided the Honours Board of Warrington RUFC for names [and names alone] to personalise my characters. My apologies all round.

The Nag's Head, a coaching inn which changed its name to the Queens Hotel at the Diamond Jubilee of 1897, did not survive the widening of Sankey Street. The Lion Hotel, a similar establishment with public rooms - one of which was large enough to be used as a courtroom and for auctions and public meetings - , survives in Bridge Street.

The modern UK rail traveller on the West Coast Main Line, speeding north after Warrington Bank Quay, follows, for a few miles, the line of our  railway. To the left are the lands once the property of the Noble Lord of our Tale and to the right lies the Parish of Winwick. My apologies to the current Baron Lilford and his kin and to today's Rector but the actions of their predecessors [3rd Baron Lilford & Rev. James John Hornby] are a matter of record. They were very much men of their time.

The Warrington & Newton Railway can lay claim to a first in that its northern link in what is now Earlestown may very well be the world's earliest main line railway junction. Perhaps as our Sir George envisaged, the line seems to have had a rather chequered career in its short independent existence until – in another possible first – it was taken over by the Grand Junction Railway in June 1835.

In attempting to furnish an authentic background, I am indebted to these works:
*Crewe to Wigan;* Adrian Hartless; [Middleton 2017]
*Crewe to Carlisle*; Brian Reed; [Ian Allan 1969]
*Railways and Waterways to Warrington (2nd Edn.)*; Peter A Norton;[Cheshire Libraries & Museums 1984] and to the *All Things Warrington* website for information on the Nags Head.

I must also thank the staff at Warrington Libraries for their courteous response to my telephone enquiries.

**OTHER TIMES, OTHER PLACES** is a book based on the unique diaries kept by two unremarkable, young Scots at two different times on two different sojourns in two different continents in the 1930's. The two Scots are the author's Mum and Dad whose observations of travel to and life in Western Australia and then Sierra Leone give a fascinating glimpse of a vanished era. The modern reader is given a picture of the background of both Diarists in industrial central Scotland and of the society which shaped their attitudes to the pioneering culture where they found themselves. Acclaimed for its comprehensive research and explanatory notes, the book includes hitherto unpublished sketches and rarely seen photographs and the cooperation of Family and Industrial Historians has enabled the inclusion of current illustrations of those scenes.

250 pp softback ISBN 978-1-787823-285-3
*[Andrew Donald Yule Imprint of CompletelyNovel.com, 2019]*

Obtainable through Amazon, Barnes & Noble etc

Royalties from the sales of this book are forwarded  to the Royal National Lifeboat Institution

========================

Coming soon [2022]

*Good Evening, Sir George*

www.ingramcontent.com/pod-product-compliance
Lightning Source LLC
Chambersburg PA
CBHW060558100726
47907CB00005B/1418